PENGUIN BOOKS .
ALL OF MY HEART

Sara Naveed is the bestselling author of *Our Story Ends Here* and *Undying Affinity*. She has a master's degree in banking and finance, and works as a content head at a software firm. She lives with her family in Lahore.

You can follow Sara on Twitter (@SaraNaveed) and Instagram (@sara_naveed) or get in touch with her through her Facebook page (www.facebook.com/saranaveedwriter).

All of My Heart

SARA NAVEED

PENGUIN BOOKS

An imprint of Penguin Random House

PENGUIN BOOKS

USA | Canada | UK | Ireland | Australia
New Zealand | India | South Africa | China

Penguin Books is part of the Penguin Random House group of companies
whose addresses can be found at global.penguinrandomhouse.com

Published by Penguin Random House India Pvt. Ltd
7th Floor, Infinity Tower C, DLF Cyber City,
Gurgaon 122 002, Haryana, India

First published in Penguin Books by Penguin Random House India 2018

Copyright © Sara Naveed 2018

10 9 8 7 6 5 4 3 2 1

ISBN 9780143444749

Typeset in Sabon by Manipal Digital Systems, Manipal
Printed at Thomson Press India Ltd, New Delhi

www.penguin.co.in

Whoever you love, love them with all of your heart

Prologue

The roads of the city were wet as it had been drizzling all evening. I had been driving continuously for the past two hours and now the exhaustion was beginning to catch up. Not that I wasn't accustomed to driving for long hours. I had been driving a taxi for Uber during weekends for the last one year. I thought back to the day I moved here from Pakistan. That was three years ago. *How times flies*, I reflected. When I wasn't driving, I was out on trips for my shoots. I was a photographer by profession. After graduating from one of the top business schools in London, I had bagged a job in Standard Chartered Bank, earned decent money and started my own photography studio. Though I should note that I didn't need the Uber money, I just did it for my own leisure. Driving helped me relax. Plus, it also paid me well. At twenty-five, I had everything I had ever hoped for. However, I did not let that go to my head. I stayed grounded and humble.

In the last two hours, I'd successfully managed to complete three trips. The longer you drove, the more you earned. As I slowed down the car at a traffic signal, I received a call from Pakistan. It was my mother. I rubbed my eyes as I answered her call.

'Salaam, Amma. How are you?' I said, my eyes fixed on the road.

'Rehaan, where are you, *beta*? Still out?' she asked, her voice filled with love and concern.

'Yes, Amma,' I replied, my voice heavy with sleep. 'I'm driving.'

'*Arrey*, I don't understand why you drive. You earn well with the studio. Go home and rest.'

'Amma, I didn't come here to rest. I'm here to make money, to better our future.'

'I know, *meri jaan*, but health comes first. You need to look after yourself, only then you will be able to work.'

'Amma, don't worry. I'm totally fine,' I told her, slowly pushing the accelerator as the signal turned green.

'I'm always telling everyone here how hard-working you are. Running your own studio and then also working part-time. You're doing a lot.'

'A part-time job? Amma, why can't you just tell them that I drive a taxi in the evening?' I asked.

'How can I tell them my son drives a taxi in London just because he loves to drive? It wouldn't give a good impression here, *na*. You know how our society thinks.'

I almost shook my head in disappointment.

'Plus, I have to find a good girl for you; someone from a reputable family. People might think that's the only earning source you've got.'

'Amma, what's the harm in that? It's a common thing here. There is no need to be ashamed of it. C'mon.'

'Arrey, you don't know anything. I'm handling it, na. You just keep quiet.'

'Fine, Amma. *Acha* listen, I have to go now. I might miss a ride.'

'No more rides. Go and sleep now,' Amma said in a stern voice.

'*Haan*, haan, I'm going.'

'And one more thing, will you transfer money this week? I have to pay the bills.'

'I know, Amma. I will do it by the end of this week.'

'Take care of yourself, beta. I miss you.'

'I miss you too. Love you. Khuda Hafiz.'

'Khuda Hafiz.'

I squinted my sleepy eyes against the light as I ended the call. Amma was right. It was late and I was exhausted. I decided to turn off the app and drive straight to East London where my apartment was. As my finger was about to hit the offline button, a request for a trip popped up on the mobile phone screen. I almost felt like cancelling it. But I couldn't. I wouldn't. Zynah Malik, the name on the screen, wouldn't let me. For a few seconds, I forgot everything else and just stared at it. I forgot how tired I was or how heavy-eyed I looked. Her name was enough to take away my sleep and tiredness. It was enough to send a chill down my spine. I brought the car to a screeching halt and then hurriedly accepted her ride. I prayed it was the same Zynah I was thinking about. I was desperate to feel her presence. I couldn't wait to see her, to talk to her. It had been so long—three years to be precise. Worried that I would be late or she would cancel the ride and find another driver, I quickly started the engine and drove towards her location. She had requested the ride from north-west London—Belsize Park.

The thought of meeting her after all these years brought a nervous smile to my face. My heart thudded loudly in my chest. Nervousness, excitement and anxiety engulfed me all at once.

I killed the engine and parked the car in front of the park; my eyes peeled for her. But she was nowhere to be seen. My heartbeat quickened as I waited for her in silence. What did she look like now? Was she as beautiful as she was three years ago? Did she still apply kohl in her eyes? Did she wear the same sparkling nose ring on her pert nose? Did she talk in one breath even now? A lot of thoughts ran through my mind. Then I thought about other things. The more serious things. What was she doing in this area around midnight? Why had she called for a taxi? Where was her own car? Was she all right? The click of the car door broke my reverie. A whiff of her perfume hit my nostrils as she sat in the back seat, reminding me of our time together. How much I had missed her.

'Harrow Support Group, please. It's in north-west London,' she said in a low but businesslike tone.

I didn't know what to focus on—her strained voice or the location she had requested for. I slightly shifted the rear-view mirror so I could catch a glimpse of her face. It was a futile attempt as it was eerily dark in the car.

'Sure,' I replied hurriedly, worried that she would recognize my voice.

However, nothing of the sort happened. She neither recognized my voice nor did she bother to look in the rear-view mirror. That did not stop me from stealing glances at her. The light from her mobile phone cast a glow on her face. Curly locks fell on her face, making it difficult for me to see her expression.

'Hello?' her voice broke the silence as she answered her phone. 'Yes . . . I'm fine. I just need some time alone . . .' she said in a muffled voice. She sniffed before she spoke again, 'I'll be back home soon. Bye.'

And in the next instant, she burst into tears. My heart exploded when I heard her crying. I didn't know how to react; I didn't know what to say. The dynamics of our relationship had changed in the past few years. There was a time when I made her feel better. She found solace in my company and often said that. However, things were different between us now. And I hated myself for that. I cursed myself. I blamed myself for putting her in this situation.

PART ONE
Rehaan

A Messed-Up Life

I don't know if my life experiences during my early teens were similar to those of others of that age. Life at fourteen was dominated by the dysfunctional environment created by a worrying mother and a careless, alcoholic father. It was not new—I had survived it for as long as I could remember.

When I returned home from school, I would always hear my mother and father quarrelling with each other. My little brother, Azaan, who was eight years younger than me, used to lock himself up in his room, pretending to study. Only I seemed to know how petrified he was of the vicious fights between our parents. I used to cheer him up by playing his favourite video games with him.

My father, Akram Sheikh, had lost all his money when his import-export business went down due to a case of fraud. Now, he was down to his last savings. His income was almost insufficient to support the family and the burden seemed to have caused a permanent slump in his shoulders. This made me despise my father sometimes.

He was smart but idled away his time, content with the financial support from my mother's family. My father mostly stayed at home, often drinking into the night. My mother's family advised her to separate or seek divorce from him but she could never muster the courage to do so. My mother was afraid it would turn her into a social pariah and would rather continue to portray the false image of us being a perfect family. She was from that order which believed a woman's identity was that of a wife—forever orbiting around a husband and family life. Once a woman was married, she had no home other than that of her husband's. Even if she did separate from my father, society would continue to question her identity as a mother. Nobody would want to marry off their daughters to her sons who had been raised without a father.

My maternal relatives ensured that we didn't die of hunger. The scraps in my father's bank account were hardly sufficient to pay off our utility bills and household expenses. Shaidi Mamu, my mother's elder and only brother, bore the most of our expenses. He paid to put Azaan and me through school. He had told my mother that I shouldn't enrol for the state-certified matriculation if I wanted to study and work abroad. He'd even promised my mother that he'd send me abroad once I graduated with a bachelor's degree. Since then, my mother was impatiently waiting for me to grow up, study hard and fly abroad for a better future for all of us. I'd sworn to myself that once I had made it in life, I'd pay off the debt to Shaidi Mamu and get rid of the burden.

The credit goes to Shaidi Mamu for ensuring that I studied at such a good school. I looked forward to school every morning. It gave me an avenue for escape where

I could dump the dysfunctionality of home and catch glimpses of Zynah—the only girl on the face of this earth who held a secret power over me. I fell in love with Zynah Malik at the very first sight and forgot all my troubles. She changed me and my life without even knowing it and gave it a new meaning. I have Shaidi Mamu to thank that I got a chance to see Zynah, to know her as a person. I still vividly remember the first time I met her in school.

First Encounter

It was mid-November, and the weather had already turned cold. I still remember how cold those days were. Amma had made me wear two sweaters so I could stay warm at school. She was proud that I was studying in a school affiliated to the O-level board while children of my age from my neighbourhood went to schools that were affiliated to the state boards. A week had passed at school but no one had broken the ice and spoken to me. Perhaps the rich spoilt brats did not like to hang out with lower middle-class boys like me. My classmates belonged to rich families and were driven to school in posh automobiles. I used to stare at them and their fancy cars with fascination, wondering if one day I might also own an expensive car. I had arranged an autorickshaw for my commute to school.

One day, after I hopped out of the auto and ambled to the school entrance, I glanced upon a group of fellow students, friends seated casually at the benches placed outside the school boundary wall, puffs of smoke blowing out of their mouths. Four boys and a girl. I wondered what made her hang out with these boys and smoke with them. Why didn't she hang out with the girls of her class? As I walked towards the gate, one of the boys from the group called out to me and asked me to stop. The blood rushed to my cheeks when I turned and saw them staring at me. The girl exhaled smoke and looked at me nonchalantly. She was beautiful. My cheeks turned a deeper shade of red.

'Hey you! Yes, you! Come here,' one of the boys said.

I adjusted the backpack on my shoulders, heaved a sigh and then walked towards them.

'Uh, yes?' I said in a low, hesitating voice.

'New at school, right?' the same guy asked.

I nodded, stealing a quick glance at the girl. I wished I could observe her a bit more because her appearance seemed peculiar, quite different from the rest of the teenage girls.

'Whoever joins midterm has to do whatever we say,' the guy declared.

'What . . . do you mean?' I stammered, looking at their faces.

'Here. Take this,' he said, giving me a cigarette.

I hesitantly took it from him.

'What do I do with this?' I asked him, furrowing my brows.

'Well, you smoke it,' he said with a smirk.

'What?' I asked, flabbergasted.

'Yes. This is what you have to do. Smoke and then you pass.'

'But . . . why? I . . . I don't smoke. I never have.'

'But now you have to.'

'I can't.'

'Then admit you're a low-class loser and nothing else,' he said, gritting his teeth.

'I'm not!' I snapped.

'Then prove it.'

I asked him for the lighter and lit the cigarette. The girl looked at me with astonishment, her eyes wide open. In order to prove myself a 'decent guy' as per their standards, I was ready to do what I'd never done or tried before in my life.

I placed the cigarette between my lips and then looked at her. This gave me an opportunity to take a good look at her. She had almond-brown eyes set in a round face; her lips were full and pink; and black, loose curls hung past her shoulders. She looked at me with an amazed expression and for a moment I imagined that she wanted me to stop. I ignored the message I thought she was sending me and took a drag. But I burst into a fit of coughs. It felt as if my lungs would explode. I felt dizzy, light-headed. My condition made the boys laugh. However, she was not amused. She caught hold of my hand, snatched the cigarette from my fingers and threw it away.

'Stop it, guys! Just stop it!' she yelled.

The boys stopped laughing.

'Can't you see he is coughing? Just look at him!'

I managed to get my breathing under control and looked up.

'Are you okay?' she asked and then put a hand on my shoulder.

'Yes, yes, I am okay. Thanks,' I whispered, shivering slightly.

'I'm sorry about my friends. They love bullying newcomers. I apologize on their behalf.'

'Hey, Zee, what are you saying?' one of them complained.

She raised her hand, indicating that he should stop.

I looked at her and then back at the boy.

'You may go to your class now. And please don't tell anyone about this little incident,' she said, looking at me with pleading eyes.

'Sure. Don't worry. I wasn't planning to,' I told her.

'Great. Thanks.' She smiled.

I nodded once again and then headed towards the school building. I walked away, leaving a piece of myself behind. My heart pulsated wildly, and my breath seemed to stop. What had her smile done to me?

And It Started

I did not believe in love at first sight. However, she made me rethink my own beliefs. I had never thought that one encounter could make me fall head over heels for someone. I had seen much prettier girls before but none of them had made me go weak in my knees like she had. Apart from her beauty and intellect, there was something else about her that made me want her. I was smitten by her personality, and every day waited to catch a glimpse of her in school. After that first chance meeting, I found out that she was my classmate. I had been so engrossed in my studies that I had not noticed her and her friends earlier. I repeated her name under my breath, the name that would change my life forever—Zynah Malik.

She would enter the class surrounded by her so-called friends, chewing gum. Before taking her seat, she would glance sidelong at the class. Sometimes I would catch her attention and our eyes would meet. She would acknowledge me with a nod of her head and one of her rare, winning smiles. My heart would sink and my stomach turn somersaults. Not knowing how to react, I would hastily smile back and turn my attention towards my books. She would put her small, delicate hand over her mouth and giggle at my awkwardness.

She was one of the brightest students of our class and often I, along with other school teachers, got impressed with her witty answers. She was a genius when it came to art and craft. And the fact that she was a talented doodler and caricaturist was known across the school. Her dressing sense was also unique. Even with the school uniform on, she looked different. She wore heavy metal bracelets on one of her wrists and covered her forehead with big headbands. She always wore sneakers instead of the standard school shoes. Her casual, relaxed demeanour is what made her so attractive. Perhaps, that was one of the reasons why I liked her—why I was so fascinated by her.

After our first encounter, the boys from her group never troubled me again. I wondered if she had asked them to stop. Strangely, we never spoke—the only interaction being the occasional exchange of smiles. I wanted to speak to her. I wanted us to be friends. I wanted to tell her how I felt. But at the same time, I was scared. I did not know how she felt about me, and I didn't want to come across as too forward.

The first two years of school passed by in a flash. It had become a routine for me to sit on the bench outside the gate and wait for her to arrive in her white Mercedes-Benz. Initially, my presence would startle her and she would shoot nervous glances in my direction. But eventually she became used to me. The glances gave way to quick, shy smiles. I always wondered when we would get past these formalities and form a real friendship. To my misfortune, that never really happened. Not until we finished our O-level.

How My Luck Changed

I think I still haven't mentioned how hard-working Shaidi Mamu was. He had quit his job at a major telecom company to start his own transport business, which provided services such as cars on rent and driving lessons apart from the usual sale and purchase of second-hand automobiles. Since childhood, I was obsessed with two things—photography and cars. So, Mamu's office became my sanctuary. Every day, after school and tuition, I would go to his office to understand the operations of his business. He loved the fact that I took such keen interest in his work. He was very attached to me because he did not have a son. He always told my mother that if he had a son, he would be just like me. He was the only person who fussed over me and spoilt me.

One day, I came to his office with my report card in hand, my heart swelling with happiness. I had scored two As and three Bs in my O-level exams which was quite an achievement in my family. Shaidi Mamu was ecstatic and as a gesture of appreciation, he surprised me with a second-hand car—a 1995 Honda Civic. He knew this wasn't the model I wanted and promised to get me a brand-new car after I completed my A-level. I threw my arms around him and hugged him tightly, tears rolling down my cheeks. I could now go to school in my own car.

A few weeks later, I walked into his office and found him slumped in his chair, looking glum. When I inquired about the problem, he told me that a client had called to request for driving classes.

'Haan so, what's the problem?' I asked him, putting my bag on the chair.

'*Puttar*, our driver is on leave today. So, we have to turn down the client for now.'

'Oh no.'

'Oh yes.'

'Mamu jaan, should I go and give the driving classes?'

'What, are you serious?' he asked.

'Yes. See, I am free after my tuition classes today. I can easily give driving classes to your client until your driver comes back.'

'But you don't even have a driving license yet. I can't put you in trouble for a client.'

'Shaidi Mamu, it's just one day. I don't want you to lose a client.'

'Hmm. I still think it's risky.'

'But why? I won't venture to the outskirts. It should be all right.'

'Okay, but I will have to ask your mother.'

'Shaidi Mamu, there's no need to ask Amma. She will get unnecessarily worried. You just have to trust me.'

'*Theek hai*. You can take the Alto for the driving class. Are you sure you can handle it?'

'Don't you trust my driving skills?' I asked him.

'Of course, I do. I was the one who taught you.' He winked at me.

'Then don't worry. I'll handle it.' I smiled reassuringly.

'Okay, so here's the address. You need to pick the trainee up at 3 p.m. from here. Done?'

'Done!'

After my tuition class, I took the car from Mamu's showroom and headed straight to the trainee's house. It was located in the Cantonment area, so it took me almost twenty minutes to reach. I turned off the engine as soon as I reached the address and got out of the car to get some air. I waited outside the house for a couple of minutes but nobody came out. The slip of paper that Mamu had given me also had a contact number. I dialled it but nobody answered. I wondered if this was the right address. Disappointed, I was about to sit back in the car and leave when I heard the click of the gate. I saw Zynah come out, lost in thought, chewing gum in her mouth. She suddenly looked up and stopped in her tracks.

'You? What are you doing here?' she asked me.

'I . . . uh . . .' I didn't know how to respond.

'Yes?' She crossed her arms and examined me suspiciously.

'I came here for the driving lessons,' I told her.

'Driving lessons? You?' she asked.

'Yes,' I said.

'Are you the driver?' she asked.

'Yes,' I said resolutely.

'Oh,' she said and smiled. 'I didn't know the driving school hired such young drivers,' she said and burst out laughing.

. I looked down in embarrassment.

'So, Captain, will you teach me driving, then?' She gave me a mischievous smile, biting her lower lip.

'Wait, are you the one who wants to learn?' I asked.

'Yes, who else!'

'Oh, okay,' I said and smiled, looking down again. I couldn't believe my luck.

'Shall we go?' she asked.

Favourite Days

After the first driving session with Zynah, I realized this was the perfect way to spend more time with her. I requested Shaidi Mamu to let me continue with the classes. He did show some reluctance in the beginning, but I was able to convince him. However, I had only ten days to befriend her. Every afternoon, after my tuition class, I picked Zynah up from her house. It was supposed to be a thirty-minute class, but I usually stretched it to an hour. Soon, all our classmates got to know that I was teaching Zynah how to drive. She had proudly told them after our first session. Her friends dissed the idea in the beginning but later started to accept me. However, they still did not include me in their group. I hardly interacted with Zynah at school. She never spoke to me except for exchanging knowing glances and smiles. Surprisingly, her demeanour was completely different during our driving lessons. She rambled on about various things—her family, friends, vacations, movies and the places she desired to see. I mostly kept quiet during these 'conversations'— gentle nods and monosyllables my only contribution. But I was fascinated by her stories; by her facial expressions;

by her hand gestures. She did ask me about my life—my childhood, my family members—but I usually turned the conversation back to her because I did not like talking about myself. There was nothing extraordinary about my ordinary story.

'So, tell me about your family. How many people live in your house?' I asked her one day.

'There's me, my mother, father and elder brother. That's it. My brother doesn't live with us.'

'Where is he?' I asked, my eyes on the road ahead.

'Australia. He's settled there.'

'Oh, nice. You can take a right turn here,' I directed her.

'Oh. Sure.'

After the class, we would often stop at her favourite coffee shop where she would order a latte for herself. I, on the other hand, never ordered anything.

'Are you sure you don't want anything? I mean, I can pay for you if you don't have money,' she said one day, her face serious.

'No. No,' I responded instantly. 'It's not about money. I just don't want it,' I told her, my expression guarded.

'All right,' she said with a shrug.

I looked down in embarrassment. I did not want her to think that I did not come from a well-off family, but I kept quiet.

'C'mon, let's go back,' she said as she stood up to leave.

We stepped outside and walked towards the car.

'Where do we go now?' she asked, her delicate hands on the steering wheel.

'Nowhere. We should head back now,' I told her.

'All right.' She hit the accelerator and revved the engine.

'Zynah, can I ask you something?' I said, looking at her sideways.

'Sure,' she said nonchalantly.

'You probably have a couple of drivers at home. Why didn't they teach you how to drive?'

'My dad, you know . . .'

'No, I don't know,' I interrupted her.

She looked at me with an incredulous expression and then we both burst out laughing.

'You're funny,' she said.

'You're beautiful,' I whispered and then almost instantly regretted it.

Shit! I thought.

She looked at me in wide-eyed surprise.

'Sorry,' I muttered, biting my lower lip.

'Never mind,' she said and added, 'Yeah, so I was saying, my father wanted me to learn driving from a professional driver.'

'And you think I am professional enough?' I asked.

'Yes, so far so good,' she said and smiled.

I nodded, not able to look away from her beautiful face.

🎧

I sleepily looked at my watch—10.30 a.m. I tucked it back under my pillow and shut my eyes. It was Saturday and I could sleep till late. The door to my room was ajar and I could hear my father yelling at my mother. I pulled the blanket over my face, hoping to go back to sleep when I saw Azaan near the bookshelf, shuffling through my things.

'Hey, what are you up to?' I asked him, sitting up in my bed.

'Bhai, I'm looking for your English dictionary. Can't find it outside. Is it here?'

'Azaan, don't disturb me. Don't you see I'm sleeping? I'll get up later and find it for you. Now go outside and shut the door!' I said, and covered my face with the blanket once more.

As I was drifting off to sleep, my cell phone beeped. It was a text message from Zynah:

Hey, can you come and pick me up earlier today? Around 12?

We had exchanged numbers right at the beginning but had never sent each other messages before this. I hurriedly got up and ran towards the washroom. Azaan looked at me with a puzzled face.

'What's the hurry?' he asked but I slammed the door shut.

After a quick bath, I wore my favourite pair of denims and a dark-blue turtleneck sweater. I quickly dried my hair and ran down the stairs.

'Rehaan?' Amma called out just as I was about to step outside.

'*Jee*, Amma?' I turned around to look at her, the car keys dangling from my fingers.

'Where are you going?' she asked, looking at the keys. 'You've not even had breakfast.'

'Amma, remember the client who is taking driving lessons? Well, she has asked me to come earlier today,' I told her the truth. There was nothing to hide. It was not like I was going to meet my girlfriend. It was pure business.

'But first have your breakfast, na.'

'I'll pick something up on the way. Okay? Bye!' I hopped into the car and drove it out of the garage.

I was eager to see her, to meet her.

I picked her up at around 11.45 a.m., and then she drove us to the outskirts, far away from the hustle and bustle of the city.

We picked up pita bread sandwiches on our way as I had not eaten anything since morning. She parked the car on the side of the road and stepped out. She was wearing black stockings with an oversized maroon cardigan and knee-length boots. She walked up to the bonnet of the car and sat cross-legged on it even as she unwrapped her sandwich. I stood beside her, eating slowly, looking at the view in front of me.

'What do you want to be when you grow up?' she suddenly asked, licking a speck of sauce off her lips.

I turned to look at her.

'Grow up? Are we still toddlers?' I laughed at my own joke.

'Ugh. C'mon. Everyone has dreams. You know. Something you'd like to achieve.'

I want you. That's my dream. For now, I thought, smiling to myself. I wished I could say that to her but kept my thoughts to myself.

'Well, if that's what you're asking . . . I want to be a photographer, a professional photographer. I have always been fond of taking pictures. In fact, I want to go abroad and study photography but I can't,' I said, sighing heavily.

'Why?'

'My family wants me to become a banker or a financial analyst.'

'How boring!' she said, her face twisting into a grimace.

I nodded, looking away.

'So, photography, huh? Wow. That sounds great. Do you have a camera?' she asked.

I laughed.

'Yeah but I don't have a DSLR,' I told her.

'Any other then?'

'Yeah, I have a digital camera in my bag,' I said, waving my hand in the air.

'Oh, great. Will you take a picture of me? Basking in the sunlight and smoking a cigarette?' she laughed.

'Are you sure?' I looked at her in wide-eyed surprise.

'Of course, I am.' She quickly opened her bag and took out a pack of cigarettes.

I walked towards the boot of my car to get my backpack. After rummaging through the books, I finally found my camera and walked back to Zynah.

'Is this pose good enough?' she asked, looking directly at me. There was a cigarette between her lips and she turned her head to look ahead—her eyes distant and faraway.

'Perfect,' I said and smiled.

'Make sure I don't look fat in it.'

I smiled to myself as I clicked the picture.

'Show me, show me!' She tried to take the camera.

'Wait, wait.' I sat down next to her and showed her the picture.

'Wow. Ah-ma-zing! You indeed know how to take a good shot!'

'Really?' I turned to look at her.

'Yes, dude.' She gave me a light pat on my back.

Her touch sent a shiver down my spine, and I almost blushed.

'In fact, you should apply to a college somewhere abroad to study photography.'

'I wish it was that easy,' I sighed.

'Listen, it's easy. Nothing is impossible or complicated. Only people make it complicated.'

I looked away, my eyes downcast.

'I want to see you as a professional photographer. You get it? Now that's my dream!'

I laughed at her.

'I'm serious!'

'Okay, okay. Now, tell me. What's your dream?'

'I just told you!'

'The real one.'

'I'm not that ambitious. I guess I just want to live freely, happily.'

'Aren't you living a free life now? Aren't you already happy?' I asked her.

'I am but I want to live on my own. Independently, you know. I want to earn my own money. As far as taking up a profession is concerned, I think I'd go for interior designing.'

'Hmm. Sounds cool,' I nodded.

She turned to look at me and smiled.

The Invitation

Rumours about our growing friendship soon spread like wildfire. One day, Ahmed, my only good friend in school, asked me about the whole situation.

'What did you do, man? I thought Zynah never gave you any attention,' he asked.

'Well, to be honest, I thought the same. I guess luck got us together. Neither of us made an effort to be friends. Everything happened on its own. I volunteered to take driving lessons for Mamu's company and then later found out that the client was none other than Zynah,' I told him.

'Awesome! Are you friends?'

'Um, I don't know. We have never discussed it.'

'The way she's been telling everyone about her new driving instructor, it seems she already considers you her friend. Otherwise she would have never mentioned it to anyone.'

'Yeah, maybe,' I said.

'Or . . .'

'Or what?'

'Or maybe she's trying to embarrass you by telling everyone that you're nothing to her but a driving instructor.'

His words hit me hard.

'What?'

'Yeah, man. I'm just telling you to be careful. These rich people can be really mean sometimes.'

I considered what he had said. Why had I never given any thought to this before? What if she had never considered me her friend but only an ordinary driving instructor?

I strolled down the corridor with these thoughts crowding my mind. I stopped in front of my locker to collect a few books.

'Rehaan!' a sweet, melodious voice called me from behind.

I turned around to find Zynah standing across the corridor.

'What's up?' she asked even as she walked in my direction.

'Nothing much. I have a class to catch. I'll see you later,' I said, not looking her in the eye.

I hurriedly locked the locker, my fingers shivering. I knew I was upset with her, but I was not sure if I could confront her. Before I could walk away, she grabbed my arm.

I was surprised at her behaviour.

'What?' I snapped at her.

'You can't walk away from me like that,' she replied, her face solemn.

'Why not?' I asked.

'It's my birthday tomorrow. I wanted to invite you,' she said, as she let go of my hand.

'Why me?'

'Excuse me?' she asked.

'Yeah. Why do you want to invite me?' I asked her, crossing my arms.

'I'm inviting all of my friends. C'mon.'

I was stunned to hear her reply.

'Am I your . . . friend?' I asked, narrowing my brows.

'Of course, you are! What made you doubt that?'

'Nothing.' I smiled at her. I was relieved.

'So, will you come?'

'Yes, I will,' I nodded.

'Awesome! Tomorrow 5 p.m. at my place then. See you!' She tapped my shoulder lightly before walking away.

I stared at her till she was out of sight and then smiled to myself.

After school, I went straight home. A lot had to be done before the party and there wasn't much time. First, I needed to decide what I would wear. I opened my cupboard and pulled out all my clothes. I pinched myself even as I picked out my shirts. It was hard to believe that she had invited me. She considered me her friend. Her friend. The thought made me smile.

It suddenly hit me that I hadn't decided what I would give her. I did not have enough money to buy an expensive gift but I did not want her rich friends to pick on me for getting a cheap one. Since she loved the photograph I'd taken of her, I decided to frame it for her.

The Party

I wore a black suit to Zynah's birthday party. Amma had had it stitched a year ago for me to wear at my cousin's wedding. I wasn't sure if I should have worn it but Amma insisted. She wanted me to be the most handsome boy there. I couldn't understand why. I thought that girls went for rich guys, not good-looking ones. Not that I thought that I was very good-looking, just average. This truth hit me harder when I stood in front of the mirror, clad in the suit.

I had spent a lot of time in packing Zynah's birthday gift the night before the party. So, I was careful with it and placed it gently next to me in the car. I hoped that she would like it. The party was to begin at 5 p.m., but I went half an hour early.

The gate to Zynah's house was open and I saw that some of the guests had already started to arrive, pulling up in their lavish cars. I parked my modest, second-hand Honda Civic at the far end of the road, away from the luxury cars, and walked to the house. A tent had been erected on the lawn, which had been decorated with fairy lights. I scanned the lawn and spotted a few of Zynah's friends from our class. They threw shocked glances at me, as if it was hard for them to believe that I had also been invited to the party. The lawn was abuzz with chatter—some were discussing their big businesses, others rattled on about their shopping plans and discussed plans for their foreign holidays. Their superficial banter made me smile to myself. I wondered who amongst these were Zynah's parents.

I was holding Zynah's gift close to myself, making sure that it was safe.

'Rehaan!' Zynah called out to me from across the lawn.

She was a vision. I'd never seen her dressed as a girl before. She had chosen an ethnic dress for the evening—a pink and orange salwar-kameez set.

'I am so glad that you've come!' she said, her kohl-outlined eyes sparkling.

Her lips, made prominent with a luscious shade of pink lipstick, stretched into a smile. I couldn't take my eyes off her.

'What happened?' she asked, as I continued to stare at her without responding to her greeting. 'Don't I look nice? Or are you also going to make fun of me like my other friends?'

'No. No. No. Zynah, you look . . . beautiful,' I said.

She blushed and tucked a few loose strands of hair behind her ears.

'Happy birthday,' I said and handed her the gift.

'Why did you bring this, Rehaan? It wasn't necessary,' she said, but took it from me.

'I hope you like it.' I smiled.

She smiled back. I kept thinking how beautiful she looked.

'Come, let's go meet the others,' she said, grabbing my arm and pulling me away with her. I towed behind her, happy as a lovesick puppy.

One by one, she introduced me to her friends. I already knew all of them since they were in my class, but I wasn't friends with any of them.

The lawn started to fill with more guests. Zynah excused herself from her circle of friends and went to greet the new arrivals, leaving me there. I did not want to engage with them and kept quiet but one of them tried to strike up a conversation with me.

'Rehaan, are you the person who is teaching Zynah how to drive?' asked Salman.

I did not respond.

'What do you mean, Salman? Are you saying that he is Zynah's driver?' Javeria asked.

'Yes. He is her driver,' Salman said, the sarcasm dripping from his words. The rest started to giggle.

'That is the best job Zynah could have offered someone like Rehaan,' Javeria said, and lapsed into another fit of giggles.

My cheeks reddened with anger and humiliation. Why did Zynah have to tell her friends about our driving lessons? They made it seem as if teaching her to drive was a very menial job. I walked away, their words still ringing in my ears. I saw Zynah talking to someone. The smile on her face faded when she saw my expression.

'What happened?' I could make out the words she mouthed, an expression of concern on her face. I did not reply. I felt the tears well up in my eyes and before they could start to stream down my face, I turned towards the exit.

'Rehaan! Wait! Rehaan!' I could hear Zynah call out to me several times from behind but I did not slow down my pace or stop. I hurried towards my car.

'Rehaan! I am asking you to stop right now!' Zynah's voice had now taken an angry tone.

I gulped back the tears and turned to look at her.

Zynah walked over to where I stood.

'What happened, haan? What's the matter? Why are you leaving so soon?'

'I need to go, all right. I need to go,' I said, not looking into her eyes.

'But why?' She caught hold of my arm and made me look at her. 'What happened?'

'Did you tell your friends that I am your driver?' I asked, not being able to control myself.

'What?' She seemed shocked.

'Yes. That's what I am to you, isn't it? A driver.'

'It's . . . it's not like that. It's not true,' she whispered, almost in disbelief.

'It is true, Zynah, it is true,' I said. I couldn't help the tear that managed to escape my eye and rolled down my cheek.

'No . . . not at all. Come here,' she said, pulling me close and wrapping her arms around my neck.

My heart decided to take a break from work, my knees shook, my tongue dried up—the world as I knew it screeched to a deafening halt.

'Both of us know what you mean to me,' she whispered, still holding me in her arms.

I managed to scoop some air into my lungs, my arms limp down my sides. I wanted to hold her too but I didn't know if I should.

'What do I . . . mean to you, Zynah?' I ventured. The break seemed to have rejuvenated my heart, which was now beating faster than it ever had.

Still holding me, Zynah arched her torso back and stared into my face. Her face was a few inches from mine, I could feel her breath on mine. Her arms still hung around my neck. She cocked her head to a side and leaned her face closer to mine. She closed her eyes, I closed mine, my heart taking its beating business to a new level. Her soft lips clasped mine and pulled at them ever so gently and then let go.

This was the first time a girl had kissed me. When I opened my eyes, the lights had dimmed around me and everything was out of focus, except Zynah's face. She was looking at me. She relaxed the grip of her arms on my neck and took a few steps back. She tucked the loose strands of hair behind her ears and then turned her gaze away. I did not know what to make of the situation. She looked nervous. Tiny bolts of electricity fired at each of my nerve endings. The nervousness on her face relaxed into a smile, which I returned. She turned around and walked away with measured steps. In our first meeting, Zynah had stolen a piece of my heart, now she had all of it. I wondered if she even knew it, as I saw her disappear into the crowd.

The Unexpected

I woke up groggy the next morning, unable to open my eyes. I could hear Amma and Abba yelling at each other. She'd asked him to pay the overdue telephone bill to which he replied that he didn't have the money. As I got out of bed, I realized I had a splitting headache. I rubbed the back of my head with my hand, trying to get rid of the pain. It did not work. The highlights of Zynah's birthday party last night flashed in front of my eyes. I had left the party with mixed feelings. I had been humiliated by Zynah's friends and felt hurt by their jibes, almost on the verge of crying. Then, Zynah had followed me out to stop me from leaving and when I asked her what I meant to her, she had responded by kissing me. I touched my lips and realized I was smiling.

'What's up, bhai? What's with the smile, haan?' Azaan asked, teasing me.

'Nothing,' I said and threw a pillow at him.

I took a shower and quickly dressed for school. I was looking forward to seeing Zynah. I had a lot of questions after last night. She had kissed me. Were we more than friends? I wanted to know what she had to say.

I parked my car at the school parking lot and headed towards my class and her. I didn't spot her in the English class. Perhaps she was not in the class yet. I plonked down on my seat and looked around. I saw her friends on the back benches. Zynah was not with them.

I realized that her driving classes were also over. It meant that I would not meet her that day. I did send a few text messages to her phone but she did not reply. I was worried if she was ignoring me deliberately or if something was wrong. I contemplated asking her friends but rejected the idea. Those who considered me a driver would not tell me anything about her.

'Rehaan, why do you look so messed up?' Ahmed asked me during recess.

'I don't know. I don't know where she is,' I told him, biting into my nail.

'C'mon, dude. She must be at home today. Perhaps resting? These rich people's parties last till late in the night. She must have danced all night and is now sleeping till late.'

I considered what Ahmed had said and then tried to change the subject.

'Maybe you're right. Let's forget about it. I have to revise for the test.' I picked up my textbook and started to read.

'Yeah, we better do that.'

I sent her a few more text messages in the evening while I was at Shaidi Mamu's office. There was still no reply. Finally, at night, I mustered some courage and gave her a call. The phone rang at first and was then switched off. It seemed unusual to me. All I could do was to wait till the next day and see if she showed up at school.

However, Zynah did not come to school all of the next week. Finally, my patience ran out and I asked her friends.

'Why isn't she coming to school?' I asked Salman and Javeria during the lunch break.

'Who?' Salman asked nonchalantly.

'You know whom I am talking about.' I crossed my arms.

'Zynah?'

'Yes.'

'You don't know? We thought you were her friend.' He started laughing.

I crossed my brows in confusion.

'Well, we're sorry about the other night. We didn't mean to offend you. Zynah didn't like it when we joked about you. She was angry with all of us. So yeah, sorry about that,' Javeria said, pursing her lips together.

I was happy that Zynah had gone to her friends and asked them to apologize to me. I felt like hugging her at that moment.

'It's fine. Can you tell me where she is?'

'She's moving to London with her family. Their flight departs tomorrow.'

'What?' I said. I felt the words suck the life out of my body.

'We thought she told you,' Salman said with a tone of surprise in his voice.

'No, she didn't,' I said.

'Doesn't matter, mate. It's not like you can do anything about it. She's leaving anyway.'

The Goodbyes

How could she just leave for London without even telling me about it? She never told me of her family's plans to move though we had spent so much time together. I drove to her home. I did not care what time of the day it was or if I was making the right choice in going there. I simply had to meet her before she moved far away from me.

I parked my car, and was greeted by a guard outside the gate.

'Jee Sahib, whom do you want to meet?' he asked me.

'Zynah . . . I want to meet Zynah,' I said, out of breath in my rush.

'Why do you want to meet?'

'I'm her friend. I used to give her driving lessons. Don't you remember me? Now, please let me go in.'

He blocked my way, putting an arm in front of me.

'Listen, please, let me go in. I need to talk to her!' I raised my voice and he backed a few steps.

'What's going on outside?' A middle-aged man in pectacles, probably Zynah's father, stepped in. 'Who is is guy, Bashir?'

34

'Sahib Jee, he is asking for Zynah bibi,' the guard told him.

'Why, who are you?' the bespectacled man asked, his eyebrows crossing into a frown.

'I'm Rehaan, Zynah's classmate and her . . . her driving instructor.'

'Oh. Why didn't you tell us earlier, young man? Come on inside,' he said, as he patted me on my shoulder and led me in. The guard glared at me as I made my way inside.

'I'm Zynah's dad, by the way,' he told me, as he gestured me to take a seat in the drawing room.

'Glad to meet you, sir.'

'Let me call Zynah. She's upstairs. Would you like to have something?'

'No, sir, thank you but I'm fine,' I said and smiled at him.

He excused himself and went outside, closing the door behind him.

The drawing room spelt luxury with heavy curtains, large and comfortable sofas and a woollen carpet. I heard Zynah's voice behind the door.

'What? Rehaan is here? Oh, my God!' she said excitedly before she opened the door to see me. I stood up. She rushed to me and opened her arms for a hug but I resisted it. A look of hurt spread across her face and the corners of her lips drooped downwards.

'Hey,' she said. The look of hurt gave way to a smile. She was not going to be dampened by my lack of enthusiasm.

'Why did you come here?'

'You never told me that you were leaving for London. Did you?' I snapped. The hurt and anger came pouring out.

'Oh, that.' She tapped her head lightly. 'I'm sorry that I didn't tell you. The plan was made suddenly. Even I found out about it last week.'

'Why didn't you tell me about it last week?'

'I don't know. It just slipped my mind,' Zynah said, shrugging her shoulders.

'How could it slip . . . why Zynah . . . why are you leaving?'

She laughed at my reaction.

'Come. Sit with me.'

We sat down on the sofa.

'Dad wants to shift his business to the UK because he has a lot of clientele over there. He feels we will have a better and more secure future in London.'

I listened to her but still none of it made sense to me.

'I will be admitted to a good college over there and perhaps land a good job after graduating. In short, I'll get to do whatever I want. You know the kind of life over there,' she said with a wink.

'Better future, right?' I asked, nodding my head.

She nodded in response.

'And what about me, Zynah? What about us?'

'What about us?' she said and shrugged her shoulders again. 'Of course, we'd stay in touch through email. I'll meet you whenever I visit Pakistan.'

'That's it?' I frowned.

'Yeah. What else?' she asked as if she had no idea what I was talking about.

'Zynah . . . are you pretending that you don't know or do you really not know?'

'What do you mean?'

'I thought . . . I thought . . .' I stammered off into silence.

'What did you think, Rehaan?'

'Zynah, I thought you had some feelings for me. The same way that I have feelings for you,' I blurted out, my eyes watering.

'Of course, I do have feelings for you. You've become one of my closest friends in such a short time.'

The phrase—'one of my closest friends'—sledgehammered my heart into grains of sand that scattered on the floor.

'A close friend? That's it?' I said, my voice cracking.

'Yes, Rehaan. You're my best friend and you know that.' Zynah patted my thigh.

'What about that . . . that night . . . that kiss . . . ?'

'Oh, that.' She tucked her hair behind her ears, gathering herself. 'Well, okay. Let's just get this straight. It was just . . . just a moment, I guess. I got carried away. I didn't realize what I was doing. You were looking so cute and I couldn't control myself,' she said, and broke into a laugh, her cheeks blushing.

I stared at her in disbelief. For her, it was just 'a moment'. The kiss hadn't meant anything to her.

'So, yeah, everything happened so quickly, I didn't get the time to think. I know it was stupid . . . '

'Okay . . . ' I interrupted her in between because I couldn't take it any more. 'I've got it . . . ' I said, standing up. 'I've got it.'

Zynah got up too and said, 'Oh, Rehaan . . . I'm going to miss you so much!' She hugged me tightly.

'I'll miss you too,' I managed to reply without breaking down. I resisted from hugging her back. She had 'friend-zoned' me and it still smarted.

'You'll email me, right?'

'Yes,' I said, my eyes ready to well up with tears.

'By the way, I love the gift you brought for me! I'm going to hang it on my wall,' she said, still hugging me.

As I walked outside her house, I wiped off the tears that had come rolling down my eyes and got inside my car. I gripped the steering wheel tight, looking at the cold, lifeless road ahead. I had lost her. I had lost my first love.

PART TWO
Rehaan

The New Life

Eight Years Later
Lahore, Pakistan

I was wearing a cream-coloured kurta, embellished with gold embroidery. I knew it looked over the top but my mother and *khalas* had made me wear it. I had graduated from the university with a leading GPA. I had not only topped my department but also bagged a gold medal. During our final semester, a few foreign universities had made a visit and offered scholarships to some of the brightest students for a master's degree abroad. Luckily, I was one of them. I was chosen for a programme at London Business School. I was ecstatic and overwhelmed. Amma was happy that her prayers had finally been heard, and she wouldn't have to ask her brother for money any more. To celebrate my achievements, she'd invited all our relatives and close friends. She had prepared a lavish spread—chicken roast, mutton karahi, biryani, seekh kebab, kheer and gulab jamuns.

The past eight years had whizzed by. I was a changed person now—not the old Rehaan. I wasn't scared to take

41

on the challenges life threw my way. I was going to live
an independent life all by myself in a new place. London,
the city of my dreams. The city where I saw myself in the
future. I thought back to the day Zynah left for London.
Zynah . . . I had not forgotten her. Even though she
had chosen to sever all ties after leaving Pakistan, I still
thought about her.

'You look dashing, bhai!' Azaan said, breaking my
reverie.

'Not as good as you,' I said, running my hand
playfully through his hair.

'Why do you always mess up my hair?' he said in an
irritated tone.

'Because you look cute with messy hair,' I laughed.

'Everybody's waiting for you outside. I think you
should stop getting ready and go meet the guests.'

'Stop acting like my big brother,' I told him, rolling
my eyes.

As I made my way outside, I saw my relatives looking
at me with admiration. My young female cousins giggled
as I walked past them. I couldn't stop myself from smiling
back at them.

I found Amma in the kitchen, setting burfi on a tray.
I hugged her from behind.

'Rehaan . . . beta, where were you? Why are you so
late? You know guests are waiting for you.'

'I know, Amma. I'm sorry,' I said.

'Acha, *chalo*, leave me now. There's so much I have
to do.' She pushed me away and directed our maid to
carry the trays outside.

I made a face. I did not want to go outside and sit and
talk to our relatives.

'Rehaan, come, beta!' Amma called me.

'Coming . . .'

I saw Shaidi Mamu sitting in a corner, talking to my other uncles. He turned to look at me and then flashed me a warm smile. His face glowed with pride. I was overcome by nostalgia for the time I had spent with him in his office, poring over automotive journals and discussing various business possibilities. He had been a father figure to me.

I suddenly realized that I had not seen Abba all morning. I scanned the room and found him sitting all alone, lost in thought. My maternal family wasn't fond of him. They believed it was a bad decision to let their daughter marry such an incompetent person. Abba, oblivious to my presence, looked at everyone's faces, pretending to be happy. He had changed considerably in the last eight years. He had restarted his import-export business and had done his best to provide for his family. Our financial conditions had slightly improved.

'Abba . . .' I called out.

'Hmm?' he turned to look at me.

'Have you had lunch?' I asked him.

'Yes, I did, son. You should have it too.'

'Sure,' I said and walked away.

Only a week was left for my departure. Amma was almost done with my shopping. She had packed jars of achar and packets of dry fruits too and had asked me to eat them regularly. I knew I was going to miss her. This was the first time I was going away from my family. Amma did try to put up a brave front, but I knew deep down she was unhappy. Shaidi Mamu understood me. He told me to come back to Pakistan if I couldn't adjust there. He even said he would give me the seed money to start my own business in case I decided to return after finishing my degree. But that's not what I had planned. Though I had got a scholarship to study finance, I still wanted to pursue photography. To chase my dreams and live comfortably in London, I had decided to study during the day and work at night. This was the only way to survive in a foreign country.

'Will you miss us, bhai?' Azaan asked as we lay in our beds the night before I was to leave.

'Of course, I am going to miss you. I'm going only for you and Amma; to better our future.'

'Acha, listen, do not forget to send me a new PlayStation as soon as you reach.'

'I will send you one as soon as possible.'

'I'll miss you,' he whispered.

'Me too,' I said, tears rolling down my cheeks.

I tossed and turned in my bed for a while but still couldn't fall asleep. Finally, I gave up. I slipped my feet into my slippers and walked towards the kitchen to get a glass of water. I was surprised to see Abba sitting all by himself in the living room. I stepped closer to check on him.

'Abba . . . you're still up?'

On seeing me, he sat up with a jerk. He instantly turned his face away to wipe his tears.

'Yes, I woke up for namaz,' he told me, avoiding eye contact.

I could sense that he was upset and this surprised me. I had never thought that my decision to go abroad would affect him like this. I stepped closer to his chair and sat on the floor beside him. I took his hand in mine and looked at him. For a moment, he seemed taken aback.

'I know your heart is heavy with guilt because you haven't been able to provide for us,' I whispered. 'I would be lying if I said I wasn't angry with you. I was angry because I wanted you to do what Shaidi Mamu did for me. I wanted you to pay for my school and university. All my life I've felt only hatred for you,' I said, a slight tremble in my voice.

Abba looked at me helplessly, tears forming in his eyes.

'Despite everything . . . I know you have tried. If you hadn't faced any troubles back then, maybe our lives would have been different.'

Abba nodded, not looking at me.

'Abba, I would not say it's all your fault. It happens. Such is life.'

He looked at me and nodded, tears rolling down his cheeks.

'I may ignore the fact that you couldn't look after our needs, but I won't ignore the way you treat my mother. Abba, please, while I am away, I expect you to treat her with respect.'

'I won't. I promise,' he said.

'I hope you're proud of me, Abba.'

'Of course, beta,' he said, taking my face in his hands. 'I am very proud of you. I want you to do what I couldn't. Make your mother proud.'

I looked at him and smiled.

'And forgive me. I wish I could have given you a better life.'

I took his hand in mine and pressed it firmly.

'Like I said, it's not all your fault. You tried your best. Sometimes good things happen to bad people and bad things happen to good people. Life is cruel. The only way to survive is to keep fighting and not give up.'

Abba nodded and leaned forward and hugged me.

'I need you to take care of my son. Okay?'

'I will. Take care of yourself and our family,' I told him.

The New Chapter

London, UK

I sat up with a jerk as the aircraft approached touchdown at Heathrow Airport. It was dark outside and I could see the runway lights glimmering below.

Shaidi Mamu had already spoken to one of his friends based in London to help me get accommodation. Rahim, his childhood friend, had arranged for an apartment in East London that I would be sharing with another person. He had asked me to download an app called Uber—a newly introduced taxi service—as soon as I reached the airport, and to book a cab to reach the apartment. I followed his instructions carefully and was soon in a homebound taxi. I was really impressed with the technology, and made a mental note to discuss it with Shaidi Mamu.

As the taxi exited the airport, I rolled down the window and let the wind gush in while I feasted my eyes on the London landscape. I called my family to inform them that I had reached. Amma was almost in tears on hearing my voice. Thankfully Azaan intervened and calmed her down.

The driver dropped me off outside the apartment building. I dragged my suitcase across the road and stepped on to the porch. No one responded to the first knock on the door, so I knocked a few more times. I wondered if the address was correct, double-checked it, resumed knocking and was just about to give up when someone yanked open the door.

'Are you Rehaan Sheikh?' a drowsy voice asked.

A man with a handsome face had opened the door. He was wearing a pair of shorts and a loose V-neck vest.

'Uh, yes. That's me,' I told him, heaving a sigh of relief.

'Cool. Come in,' he said, yawning.

I made my way into the apartment, which had cream-coloured walls adorned with ivory curtains. A plasma-screen TV was affixed to one of the walls and the bookshelf next to it was stuffed with books of all sizes. A three-seater couch with colourful cushions was at the centre of this lounge. I kept my backpack on the floor while I took in the decor.

'Your room is upstairs. You can put your stuff there.' The guy, probably my flatmate, picked up my backpack and threw it back at me.

I was startled at his odd behaviour. He did not offer to help me carry my luggage to the room, so I picked it all up and started climbing the stairs. The room assigned to me was not all that bad. It was small, the walls painted a sky blue, except for one which was a floor-to-ceiling window. A wooden cupboard and a study table occupied the remaining corners. I drew the curtains and leaned over the windowsill to get a better view of the road below.

'Dude, are you hungry? Do you wanna eat something?' a voice called out from behind.

Startled, I turned around to find my flatmate standing at the door, a bowl of spaghetti in his hand.

'No, thanks. I'm fine,' I said.

'Sure?'

'Yeah.'

'I am Vikram, by the way. I own this place,' he said with a wave of his hand.

'Oh. Nice to meet you, Vikram. I'm Rehaan.'

'I know. You've come from Pakistan. I'm Indian. Hope that's not a problem?'

'Oh, no. No. Not at all,' I said with a smile.

'Cool. I hope you're already aware of the payment terms and conditions?'

'Yes, I know,' I said with a nod.

'Cool. See you around then,' he said, closing the door behind him.

I hurriedly took out my DSLR—a priceless possession I had purchased from my savings—and took a picture of the view in front of me. I smiled when I saw the results in the small camera screen.

I don't know when I fell asleep. When I woke up, the room was engulfed in darkness. I checked my mobile phone to see what the time was. I had slept for three hours straight. My stomach growled with hunger. I got off the bed, straightened my clothes and made my way outside. I could hear blaring music from the living room and wondered if Vikram was still around.

'Vikram?' I called out, but there was no response.

I made my way downstairs and entered the living room. There was no one in sight. The TV was on but nobody was watching it. I looked around and finally found the kitchenette. I opened the fridge to see if there was something to eat. I found a can of orange juice. I couldn't find a clean glass, so I drank directly from it.

It was eerily quiet inside so much so that the hum of the refrigerator was distinctly audible. I shuddered a little as I threw the empty can in the dustbin and then hurried back to my room. As I crossed Vikram's room, soft moans of pleasure caught my attention. I stepped closer to the door and then took a step back as the bed suddenly squeaked. I knew what was going on inside. I trembled a little and my cheeks turned a deep crimson. I almost ran to my room and quickly shut the door.

I woke up early the next morning as I did not want to be late on my first day. I quickly took a shower and put on a pair of faded jeans and a grey pullover. As I made my way towards the staircase, I noticed that Vikram's door was ajar. I wondered where he had gone at 8.30 a.m. I realized I should hurry and ran down the steps but stopped abruptly as I reached the kitchenette. A pretty girl, dressed in a loose shirt that hung over her bare shoulder and denim shorts, was sitting at the counter, sipping milk directly from a carton.

'Hi,' she said in a husky voice.

I simply nodded at her and turned my gaze towards the refrigerator which was still slightly open. I opened it and took out another carton of milk and poured some in a glass.

'You want me to make breakfast for you?' she asked, leaning over the counter.

I was slightly surprised at her question. Why would she make breakfast for me?

'Hmm?' she waited for my response.

I was busy checking her out. She looked sensual in those night clothes. I gulped a mouthful of milk before replying. 'No, thanks,' I said, looking at my wristwatch.

'By the way, I'm Avantika. Vikram's . . .'

'By the way . . .' I cut her in between. 'I am getting late. Maybe we can catch up later? Take care. Bye,' I said putting the glass on the counter.

London Business School was located on the northwest side of the city. After a ten-minute walk, I reached Westminster Station. From there, I took the Tube to Baker Street Station. It was a ten-minute walk from here to the university. As I walked down the cobbled street, I couldn't stop marvelling at the beauty of the city. The architecture of LBS was stunningly beautiful. As I entered the campus, I noticed there was a sports centre, a restaurant, three cafés and a library all under one roof.

As I made my way inside the university, I was blown away with its sheer elegance and beauty. One part of the university was still under construction, which indicated it was soon going to expand. I asked one of the students for directions to the office. The administrator gave me a few forms to fill and then congratulated me for getting a scholarship. There were only a few from my country who had got this opportunity.

'Thank you,' I said. 'Uh, are there any extracurricular clubs I can be a part of? A media club?'

'Yes, there are,' the administrator told me.

'I want to join the photography club, if there's any.'

'There is one. I'll add your name to the members' list so you can be notified of the upcoming sessions. Welcome to LBS,' she said, smiling.

'Thank you.' I smiled back at her, feeling giddy.

The Delusion

I was glad that I was finally settling down. I had classes four days a week and the other three days were booked for the media club. I talked to Amma and Azaan almost every other day on Skype. Occasionally, I talked to Abba and Shaidi Mamu too. I also kept in touch with my school and college friends through Facebook. I would tease Ahmed and ask him to shift to London so I could hook him up with a *gori*. He would laugh at my absurdity as he knew his dad would never let him come.

There were times when I seriously considered taking a part-time job to earn some extra money but both Amma and Shaidi Mamu always tried to talk me out of it. They told me I shouldn't worry about the expenses and should only focus on my studies. I didn't like being dependent on someone else. Therefore, I decided to take up a part-time job without telling anyone about it.

My flatmate, Vikram, and his girlfriend chose to keep a distance from me, and I did the same.

I would be lying if I said that I never searched for Zynah on social media. I did stalk her on Facebook sometimes. I could only look at her display and cover

photos as most of her information was private. She still
lived in London but I had no idea in which locality. I
often fantasized about bumping into her some day.

🎧

Instead of the Tube, I had taken a bus to the university.
I regretted my decision as soon as I stepped in as it was
over-crowded. Since I did not get a place to sit, I had to
stand all the way to my stop. My backpack felt heavy
on my shoulders as it was loaded with books, a laptop,
and my camera. The bus stopped at a traffic signal and
new passengers stepped in. Yawning, I looked outside the
window. Suddenly my heartbeat quickened as I thought I
saw a familiar face standing by the side of the road. Was
it Zynah? Or was I hallucinating? It was difficult to say.
I rubbed my eyes and inched closer to the glass window.
The lights turned green and the bus jerked forward. It
soon gathered speed and I lost sight of her. I wanted to
believe she was Zynah. Who else could it be? I wish I had
jumped out of the bus. I had missed the chance. But I had
noticed the name of the music store behind her. I made a
mental note to visit the store soon.

The next few days passed rather slowly. Every day, I
took the same bus, hoping to catch a glimpse of her once
again. Unfortunately, there was no sign of her.

But my luck changed one day. I saw her. I kept my
eyes peeled as the bus stopped at the same signal again
and there she was. Dressed in a pair of torn denims, a
beige-coloured loose cardigan and brown ankle boots,
she was walking towards the music store. As I observed
her face, a sense of familiarity hit me. My heartbeat
almost stopped. I knew her. I recognized her face. She

looked exactly the same. The only difference was that she was wearing kajal. Her nose was still the same, delicate, but now a sparkling nose ring adorned it. She had grown her hair over the years; it fell beautifully in loose curls over her shoulders.

I didn't want to lose her again, so I quickly ran towards the exit door and jumped out. I noticed there was a lit cigarette between her fingers. She still had not quit smoking, I reflected. A lot had changed about Zynah but for me, she was still the same girl I had fallen in love with. I smiled at her, knowing that she wasn't even aware of my presence. I couldn't hold my excitement and happiness. I had finally found her.

The Near Encounter

Zynah was rummaging through her leather handbag. After she had found what she was looking for—a pair of earphones—she jerked her head up and turned it in my direction. I quickly hid my face behind a book. When I looked around after a few seconds, she was not at her spot. She had wandered off. I quickly crossed the road and followed her, as discreetly as possible. I wondered where she lived and if she still lived with her family. Was she still studying or had she completed her education? What if she'd settled down? What if there was someone else in her life? What if she was dating someone? Brushing off these thoughts, I tried to focus on where she was going.

She suddenly stopped in her tracks, pulled out her phone from her pocket and had a short conversation with someone. She then resumed walking, this time in the direction of the music store. I followed her like a crazy, lovesick puppy.

In the shop, she strolled through the aisles, occasionally picking up an album or two. I followed her stealthily, pretending to look at the music albums stacked in the shelves. I did not want to get caught. I did not want to come across as a stalker. Suddenly, my phone beeped and the sound distracted me. It was a message from Ahmed. I switched off my phone and quickly looked up. But Zynah was nowhere to be seen. I panicked and ran down the aisle, frantically searching for her. I was almost going to give up when I heard a titter of laughter. I turned around. There she was, standing right behind me. She had her headphones on and was swaying to the tune. I smiled, relieved to see her again. I was contemplating talking to her when I saw her checking her phone and then walking towards the door. I followed her. A silver sedan was waiting for her on the other side of the road. She crossed the street, walked towards the car and got inside. I looked on, wondering if I would ever see her again.

The Night Out

It was a Friday, and I was free. Since I didn't have any classes, I decided to take a tour around the city on my own. I looked for part-time jobs in the nearby areas on the Internet and decided to go for walk-in interviews. There was a vacancy at a convenience store just around the corner. Michelle, the owner, greeted me as I entered the store. She asked me if I had any prior experience in handling cash registers and I said no. However, I assured her that I was quite good at managing money. She seemed reluctant at first but then said she would hire me for a day to see if I could handle the pressures of the job. I readily accepted her offer. She explained the basics of the job and took me to the cash counter. A young English boy, probably around my age, was standing behind it. I shook hands with him and introduced myself. He was my colleague and Michelle asked him to show me the ropes. The day passed uneventfully, and at around 5 p.m. she called me to her office.

'I think you handled the job effectively,' she told me.

'Thanks. So . . . am I hired?' I asked nervously.

'Yes, you are. You will have to work twenty hours a week for which I will pay you 120 pounds. All right?'

I did not know how the pay scales worked in London, so I agreed to whatever she said.

'All right, great. See you tomorrow then.'

'Thank you, Michelle. See you.'

I walked home feeling tired but satisfied. I was finally going to do something on my own; earn my own money.

Vikram was sitting in the living room and Avantika was putting on a pair of high-heeled sandals when I opened the door to our apartment and stepped in.

'Hey, Rehaan. What's up?' he asked, fixing his tie.

'Hi. Nothing. I, uh, got a job,' I told them, closing the door behind me.

'Great! This calls for a party!' he said, beaming.

'Party?' I asked.

'We're going for a party. Do you wanna come with us?' he asked.

'Who is the host?' I asked.

'One of my closest friends is celebrating his birthday at a local nightclub. Do you want to come?'

'Thanks, but I'm busy. I have to finish my assignments.'

'C'mon, Rehaan. It's the weekend. Don't be so boring,' Avantika said, wrapping her bare arms around Vikram's shoulders.

'Plus, there will be a lot of girls there. Hot girls,' Vikram giggled.

I rolled my eyes.

'And . . . we need someone to click pictures. I'll ask my friend if he can pay you.'

'I don't do this for money,' I told him, feeling a bit offended.

Did he really think I would go for money?

'That's cool. Come with us, then. You'll have fun, promise,' Vikram said, putting his arm around my shoulder.

I looked at his hand and then at him.

'So, you are coming?' he asked.

'Okay,' I said with a nod.

'Great. Get ready in five minutes. We are already late.'

We walked to the club as it was only a few blocks away. As soon as we entered, Vikram and Avantika were ambushed by a group of people. I felt left out because I didn't know anybody. I left the group behind and decided to look around. I switched on my camera and started taking candid shots. The place was beautiful, full of colours and vibrant people. I looked at it through my lens—an energetic couple was swirling on the dance floor; two middle-aged men were engaged in an animated conversation; a group of teenaged girls were giggling; an attractive girl was standing alone at the bar, smoking.

'Hey!' she said and held up her hand as the flash hit her eyes.

'Oh shit,' I whispered, realizing the girl was none other than Zynah. My heart stopped beating. My face crimsoned and I went weak in my knees.

'Please don't take my picture,' she scowled.

'I know, I am sorry,' I replied quickly and then turned around. I did not have the guts to face her, let alone have a conversation with her.

'Hey, wait,' she called out to me.

I stopped. My hands trembled a little and my throat went completely dry. She walked up to me, a glass of mint margarita in her hand.

'I think I know you,' she said as she looked me up from head to toe.

'No, you don't,' I replied. 'I mean, I don't know. It must be a mistake.'

'Really? I don't think so. I mean, I'm quite sure,' she said, looking confused.

'Well, uh, excuse me,' I said, whizzing past her.

I quickly walked in the other direction. I had never imagined I would bump into her in a place like this. What was she doing here? Was she also invited? I wondered whom she had come with. I watched her from a distance but she seemed busy with other people—chit-chatting, smoking and drinking. I tried to avoid her and focus my attention on clicking pictures but I couldn't. Right then, someone tapped me on my shoulder, breaking my reverie. I turned around to see that a group of people had surrounded me.

'Umm, yes?' I asked, my voice laced with nervousness.

'Who invited you here?' one of the guys asked. He was a desi.

'I came here with Vikram,' I told him.

'Vikram? Who's Vikram?' the other guy asked.

'He's my flatmate.'

'Do you think we care?' one of the girls asked. 'It's our party, and we've only invited people we know. So just get the hell out of here.'

I felt embarrassed, shocked, hurt. I didn't know how to respond. I looked for Vikram and Avantika but they were busy drinking and chilling with others. What was I thinking? Did I really think they would come to my rescue?

'Can't you hear, young man? The girl is asking you to leave,' the guy said.

I nodded at them and turned to leave but Zynah stepped in.

'Hey, Keith, all okay?' she asked one of them.

'Yeah, Zee. We were just checking on this guy. He's been taking pictures without our permission.'

'Well, Keith, don't worry. He's with me,' she told them.

I looked at her, shocked

'Are you sure, Zee?' Keith asked, looking at me with curiosity.

'Yes, he's here with me. I know him,' she assured him.

'Okay, cool. Nothing to worry about, then. Have fun,' Keith said, and eyed me suspiciously before walking away.

Nostalgia hit me. Once again, she had saved me. Memories came flooding back as I remembered her birthday party and how she had come to my rescue there as well.

'I . . . uh . . .' I mumbled.

'It's okay. Have fun,' she said with a glare. I looked on as she disappeared into the crowd, my heart shattered into a million pieces.

The Apology

The next day, I walked to the same music store where I had seen her yesterday, hoping to see her again. I wandered through the aisles, looking at new releases. But my mind was elsewhere. Every approaching footstep, every clink of the door made my heart beat faster. Every now and then I craned my neck to see if she was here. After around half an hour, she walked into the store, wearing a pair of khaki pants and a bright pink cardigan. She looked adorable, and I couldn't stop admiring her. She walked down the aisle, checking out the albums one by one. I followed her around for a while, picking up the albums she had just held in her hands. I saw her put on a pair of headphones and I too followed suit. Soon, I got engrossed in the song I was listening to and lost track of time. When I realized that a considerable amount of time had passed and looked up, she was nowhere to be seen. I wondered if she had left.

'Damn . . . where did she go?' I whispered to myself, ruffling my hair.

'Looking for someone?' I heard her voice.

Startled, I turned around and almost bumped into her.

'Oops. Be careful,' she said.

'Sorry,' I muttered, a little embarrassed.

'So, dude, *chakkar kya hai*? Were you looking for me?' she asked me.

I tried to avoid her gaze but it was impossible.

'Or should I say . . . were you following me, stalker?'

'No . . .' I blurted out. 'It's not like that. I . . . uh . . . I'm not a stalker.'

'Then what were you doing here?'

'I just wanted to . . .'

'Yeah?'

'I wanted to apologize for the other day.'

'Oh,' she said, raising her brows.

'What I did at the party last night was really stupid but you saved me . . .' I continued.

'Why didn't you just tell me you were Rehaan?' she asked all of a sudden.

The question took me by surprise. She remembered me. My name. My face. Everything.

'You thought I'd forget you? Dude, I don't forget my friends so easily!'

I looked down, feeling embarrassed.

'How could I not recognize you? Your face! It's the same . . . You still have that innocent face,' she said, beaming.

I looked into her eyes.

'Rehaan . . .' she said. 'Where have you been, yaar? I've missed you so much!' She stepped closer and embraced me, leaving me stunned. I did not have the courage to hug her back. The intimacy of the act sent thousands of chills down my spine.

'You haven't changed much, have you?' She pulled herself back and then observed me from head to toe.

I smiled at her.

'Except for your hairstyle,' she said as an afterthought.

'Maybe,' I whispered.

'I'm soooo happy to meet you, seriously!' She patted me on my arm.

'Me too,' I told her, nodding. I meant it. I had not felt this happy in a long time.

The Perfect Conversation

She suggested we go to a nearby Pakistani restaurant, Original Lahore, for lunch and I readily agreed. She talked non-stop as we walked to the eatery from Baker Street Station, telling me about the delicacies served there. After we had settled down at our table, she called the waiter and ordered a few dishes without looking at the menu or asking me. There was no doubt that she was a regular here.

'Their mutton biryani is really good, and the chicken cheese kebabs are to die for! Have them with the green chutney,' she said after placing the order.

I didn't reply and just looked at her fixedly. She shifted uncomfortably in her chair and looked away. I realized I was making her awkward and shifted my gaze, taking in the décor of the restaurant. It was a small, cosy space with colourful furniture and kitschy wall art.

'So, tell me . . .' Zynah said breaking my reverie.

'Yeah?' I asked, looking at her

'Dude, what are you even doing here?' she asked.

'Uh, well, you brought me here for lunch, I guess,' I answered.

She looked at me with a confused expression and then burst out laughing. '

'What happened? Why are you laughing?' I asked nervously.

'Stupid, I meant, what are you doing in London?' she asked, suppressing her laughter.

'Oh, acha. Sorry. I'm doing my master's from London Business School. I got a scholarship,' I said.

'Wow,' she said, clapping her hands in delight. '*Kya baat hai*. I mean that's amazing.'

'Thank you,' I said and smiled.

'I didn't know you were the studious kind,' she said and winked at me.

'Well, then you don't know me at all,' I said, taking a sip of water.

'Hmm. Maybe. Where are you putting up, by the way?'

'I am sharing a house with another person in East London. What about you? Where do you live?'

Suddenly the waiter appeared, bearing a tray of food. He had interrupted our conversation and we waited patiently as he placed the dishes on the table.

'I live with family here. Willow Road, Hampstead,' she said as she served me rice.

'Oh, nice. Studying or working?' I asked, helping myself to the salad.

'Take the chicken kebab as well,' she said. 'I have completed my bachelor's and I'm employed in a leading interior design company.'

'Oh, wow, that's cool,' I said, between mouthfuls. 'I can't imagine you working in an office.'

'Why not?'

'I don't know.' I shrugged, smiling. 'By the way, this mutton biryani is really something.'

'See, I told you! Whenever you miss Pakistani food, just come here,' she said.

'With you?' I asked her.

'Yeah,' she said casually. 'Of course. Why not?'

I smiled at her response.

After lunch, we walked down the road towards the nearest Tube station. The sky was beginning to dusk, its colour changing from light blue to hues of orange.

'So, Zynah, what did you study in college?' I asked her, breaking the silence.

'I took up interior design as my major. That's how I landed a job at one of the biggest design companies, FK Designs, you know.'

'No, I don't know,' I said, a smile playing on my lips.

She laughed. And I laughed too.

'You're still funny,' she said, looking at me.

'And you're still beautiful,' I mumbled.

'So, uh . . .' her voice trailed off.

'So what does FK stand for?'

'Farid Kamran. That's the name of the owner.'

'Cool.'

'What about you? What do you do in your free time?'

'Well, I have got classes four days a week. Apart from that, I've got a part-time job. I've also joined a photography club at the university.'

'Wow! Photography! I almost forgot how much you loved taking pictures,' she said.

'Remember, I framed one of your pictures and gave it to you on your birthday?'

'Oh yeah, I remember,' she said absent-mindedly as her phone beeped.

'Do you . . . uh . . . do you still have it?'

She stopped to look at me.

'What happened?' I asked her.

'You know, I won't lie. But I think I left it in Pakistan,' she said, biting her lip.

'Oh, right. No problem,' I said, my voice laced with disappointment.

'I hope you will take another some day.'

'Sure, why not,' I said.

'Rehaan, for how long have you been here?' she asked me all of a sudden.

'It's just been two weeks,' I said. 'Why?'

'I'm sure you haven't been around the city. Have you?'

'Uh, no, I haven't.'

'Great!' She jumped at the opportunity. 'I'll take you on a tour then!'

'What? Are you sure?' I asked, stopping in my tracks.

'Why not! I get free from work at 5 p.m. So yeah, I'll take you.'

'Okay. When?'

'I'll text you the time and place.'

'Uh, I don't have your number.'

'Oh, yeah, you don't. Give me your phone. I'll save it.'

'Thanks,' I said.

I couldn't believe that she had herself volunteered to take me around the city. Neither of us spoke as we walked to the Tube station. I was already thinking about our upcoming rendezvous.

'Okay, time to go. I'll see you soon, then,' she said as we parted ways at the station.

'See you soon, Zynah,' I said, waving at her.

'Bye, Rehaan.' She waved back, smiling.

Truth or Dare

It was Sunday, and I planned to finish all my household chores. I started off with laundry. After a tiring morning, I had just settled on my bed and opened my laptop to Skype with Amma and Azaan, when Vikram walked in, holding a spatula.

'Hey, Rehaan, want to have some breakfast?' he asked, startling me. Once again, he hadn't bothered to knock.

'Uh, no, thanks. I'm fine,' I said.

'You sure?'

'Yeah, man. Thanks for asking though.'

Around lunchtime, I went downstairs to get something to eat. There were no leftovers in the refrigerator, and there were no groceries either. *I should have accepted Vikram's offer*, I thought regretfully. Feeling disappointed, I walked back to the living room and plonked myself on the couch. Memories of yesterday's lunch with Zynah came rushing back, bringing a smile to my lips. I took out my phone and dialled her number. My heart thumped with excitement with the ringing of the phone.

'Hi, who's there?' she answered.

'Hi, Zynah.' My heartbeat quickened. 'It's me.'

'Me, who?' she asked sarcastically.

'Rehaan,' I said, narrowing my brows.

'Who Rehaan?' she asked.

I was taken aback by her question. How could she forget me in a day? Was she pulling my leg or had she actually forgotten me? 'Zynah, it's me, Rehaan . . . your friend. We met yesterday . . .' my voice trailed off.

'Oh, shit! Rehaan! I'm so sorry, yaar . . . I was in the gym. What's up?'

'Uh, it's okay, never mind. I just got free. Was wondering if you were free today?' I asked nervously.

'Why don't you meet me at Hard Rock Café at 5 p.m. I'll be there with a few friends. Come, join us.'

'Uh . . .' I didn't know what to say.

'Rehaan?'

'Yeah?'

'Don't be shy,' she laughed. 'You're coming. See you. Bye!' she said and hung up.

Her forwardness brought colour to my cheeks, and I looked down at the phone in my hand, a smile playing on my lips. I contemplated what to do for a few minutes and then rushed up the stairs to get ready.

I reached Old Park Lane where the café was situated at 5.30 p.m. Zynah and her friends were sitting at a corner table, deep in conversation. I had never met her friends before and felt a little awkward. But then I mustered up the courage and walked up to their table.

'Hi,' I said, looking at Zynah.

Her face lit up with a warm smile on seeing me.

'Rehaan!' she exclaimed, getting up and leaning forward to give me a quick hug. 'How are you?'

'I'm fine,' I said.

'Guys, meet Rehaan. We used to study together in Pakistan,' Zynah introduced me to her friends.

'Hi, Rehaan!' the girls said in unison

'Hi,' I said, waving my hand.

'What will you have?' one of the girls asked.

'This is Soniya, my best friend,' Zynah said.

In the excitement she had forgotten to let go of my hand. And her touch sent thousands of shivers down my spine.

After we had settled down, Zynah ordered a burger for me. Soon everyone got busy talking. I contributed to the conversation occasionally but mostly kept quiet. Sensing my plight, Soniya suggested we play a game of truth or dare. Zynah agreed instantly. She rotated an empty beer bottle and as luck would have it, it stopped at me.

'So, Rehaan, truth or dare?' Soniya asked.

I looked around the table, assessing their facial expressions. Zynah eyed me curiously. I didn't want to get myself in trouble, so I chose the safer option.

'Truth,' I replied.

'Whoa!' Zynah exclaimed.

'All right. So, tell us about your first crush?' Soniya asked.

I instantly regretted my decision of choosing truth, or even agreeing to play this game. How could I tell them the truth?

'Rehaan, tell us na!' Zynah insisted.

'Uh, yeah . . .' I mumbled.

'Hurry! You can't take so much time . . .' one of them said.

'She was in my school . . .' I said, lowering my eyes.

'What? Really?' Zynah said, her eyes wide with shock.

I nodded.

'How come I didn't know about this?' she asked.

'I guess you never asked me,' I said with a nervous shrug.

'And you never told me,' she said, looking at me accusingly.

For a moment, our eyes locked.

'Please continue, Rehaan. Tell us more about her,' Soniya said, bringing me back to the present.

'Well, yeah,' I said, looking away. 'What else do you want to know?'

Suddenly, Zynah's cell phone beeped.

'Guys, wait. It's a call from home,' she said as she slid out of her seat and walked away from the table to find some quiet. My eyes followed her. I noticed she was distraught and frown lines had appeared on her forehead. I excused myself and walked up to her.

'Is everything okay?' I asked her, folding my arms.

'Mummy's getting a panic attack. I need to go home,' she said and rushed towards the door.

'Hey, Zynah!' I said, running after her. 'Do you want me to come with you?'

'Rehaan, you don't need to worry. I'll be fine.'

'I can come with you.'

'You want to?' she asked as she stopped to look at me.

'Yeah, only if you are okay with it,' I said, looking into her eyes.

'Let's go,' she said.

She stopped the car in front of her house on Willow Road, Hampstead, and ran out. I followed her. But she had already entered the house by the time I reached the gate.

I stood outside, wondering what to do. *What was I doing here? I should have gone back*. I cursed myself for coming with her.

'Rehaan!' Zynah called out.

'Yeah?' I turned around to look at her.

'Why are you standing there? Come inside!'

'But . . .'

'Come inside!'

I nodded, making my way towards the door. I took in the décor as I walked into the living room. Her house was not big but was warm and cosy. A familiar fragrance hit my nose, reminding me of our days in Pakistan.

Right then, Zynah's father came into the room. I remembered his face clearly. Except for a few strands of grey hair, he hadn't changed much.

'Daddy, is all good?' Zynah asked.

'Yeah, honey. She has had her medicine and is sleeping now.'

'Thank God,' Zynah said, heaving a sigh of relief.

'Who is this young man? I have seen him somewhere,' he said, squinting his eyes.

'Oh, I'm sorry. I forgot to introduce you to him. Daddy, this is Rehaan. We were in school together in Lahore. He has recently shifted to London for his master's programme.'

'Oh, that sounds great. Good to meet you, son,' he said, taking my hand in his.

'The pleasure is mine, sir.'

'Why don't you have a cup of coffee with us? Zynah?' he asked, and looked in her direction.

'Sure. I'll brew a pot,' she said.

'No, it's okay. I should leave,' I said.

'It's all right, beta. Come, sit with me,' Zynah's father said, pointing at the couch.

'So, for how long are you in London?' he asked, taking a seat.

'I have no idea. All depends on whether I get a job here or not,' I said.

'Great.'

'Coffee is here!' Zynah announced.

'Thanks,' I said as she handed me a cup.

'Zynah, why don't you get the cookies your mother baked yesterday?'

'Sure, Daddy,' she said, walking towards the dining room.

'So, where are you staying?' Zynah's father turned back to me.

'I'm sharing a house with another person in the East London,' I told him.

'That's a nice place. You can come visit us any time you want.'

'Thanks, sir.'

'Call me uncle, not sir,' he said, smiling.

I smiled back and nodded.

'How's the coffee?' Zynah asked me.

'It's really nice. Thanks.' After a while, I took my leave and Zynah accompanied me to the gate. There was a nip in the air, and I noticed Zynah folded her arms as she shivered slightly.

'Have you booked a taxi?' she asked me.

'Yeah, I have.'

'Okay . .   her voice trailed off.

We both remained silent for a while before she spoke again.

'I'm sorry about my mother,' she whispered as we walked down the porch.

'What are you sorry for?' I asked.

'You know, my mother and her stupid panic attacks. She gets worried for no reason.'

'May I ask something?'

She nodded.

'Why does she have these panic attacks?'

'I don't know. I mean, it's all my brother's fault.'

'Why, what's wrong?'

She sat down on the steps outside her house and I followed suit.

'It all started when he decided to settle down in Australia with his wife and not here with us. She misses him.'

'Why doesn't he move here?' I asked.

'His wife won't let him. She's not really fond of us.'

'That's bad,' I said, making a face.

'Yeah, very bad,' she said and pretended to laugh.

'I hope your mother feels better.'

'Oh, it's okay. Doctors have told her multiple times to take it easy. Sometimes, I think she does this on purpose, maybe to seek my brother's attention. Whenever she gets a panic attack, my brother gets worried and starts calling her.'

I chuckled softly.

'Anyway, what are you doing tomorrow?' she asked, changing the topic.

'I have college. I'm free after 3 p.m.'

'Oh God . . . I have work tomorrow!' she said, hiding her face with her delicate hands.

She looked adorably cute sitting there on the steps, the evening sun casting a warm glow on her face. I looked away as my phone beeped—the taxi had arrived.

'So, when will I see you next?' I asked as I stood up.

'I'll try to get done earlier tomorrow so that I can take you around.'

'Are you sure?'

'Of course!' she said, wrapping her arm around my shoulder. 'Dude, you're in my city. It's my responsibility to show you the real London!'

'All right,' I said, looking at her. 'See you tomorrow then.'

'See you,' she said, waving her hand.

London City Tour

I was in the hallway when a poster hung on the noticeboard caught my attention. It was a promo for a photography session in Seattle, Washington. The winner would be awarded a certificate in photography from the University of Washington. Interested candidates had to submit a few of their best photographs to the given email address. I rushed to the computer lab and switched my laptop on. I chose some of my best shots, attached them to an email I drafted and sent it to the submission email ID mentioned on the promo poster. I secretly prayed for my pictures to get selected. My thoughts were interrupted by the cell phone buzzing in my pocket—it was Zynah. She asked me if I was free. I did not have any plans and even if I did, I would have dropped them immediately to spend time with her. She told me to meet her outside the same music store around 4 p.m. I packed the laptop back into my backpack, zipped it shut, headed out of the university and caught the Tube on time. Zynah was waiting for me on the bench outside the music store. As usual, she had earplugs stuffed in her ears, shutting out the world around her.

'Hey,' I said once I was close enough to her.

'Oh, hi,' she said, removing the earplugs from her ears.

'What's up?' I asked. 'What's the plan?'

'Here's the plan,' she got off the bench and said, holding up two plastic cards at me. 'I've got two London Passes.'

'How do they work?' I asked, taking one from her.

'A London Pass is a sightseeing pass. Well, it's more like a pass to the city's top attractions that requires less of our time for research and is cheaper than trying it ourselves.'

'Wow! How long have you been planning this?' I asked, surprised.

'Planning what?' she asked.

'This sightseeing trip?'

'Dude, I just bought them last night,' she said and nudged me playfully.

I threw my head back and laughed.

'You don't have to laugh. This is a fun thing. Once you have this card with you, you won't have to pay separately to access the attractions and sights included in this pass. Gotcha?'

'Gotcha,' I said with a nod.

'Let's start with the hop-on and hop-off bus tour.'

'Cool.' I felt a surge of happiness inside me as we walked to the bus stop.

We literally hopped on to the double decker bus and saw several of London's tourist spots from the comfort of our seats as the bus drove through the city's streets. This was the best chance to capture London's essence through my lens. I fished the camera out of my bag and started taking photographs. The bus passed the Tower of London, Buckingham Palace, Tower Bridge, Big Ben and Trafalgar Square. I could not believe that I was touring the city with Zynah by my side. While taking photographs of the landmarks on my camera, I also took candid photographs of Zynah, and she looked beautiful in all of them.

She caught the lens pointed at her and said, 'Hey, what are you doing?'

'Nothing, I was just taking pictures of Big Ben,' I lied.

'Are you sure?' she laughed.

'Yeah,' I nodded. 'I'm sure.'

'Should I check your camera?' she said, looking at me from the corner of her eyes.

I laughed, looking away.

Later in the evening, after we had hopped off the bus, she took me to one of her favourite places in North London—St Pancras Old Church. I wondered why she had brought me there. Had she secretly changed her faith to Christianity?

'Zynah, why exactly are we here?' I asked her as we approached the entrance of the church.

'It's quite peaceful here, Rehaan. I'm sure you'll love it.'

'But it's a church,' I reminded her.

She stopped midway to look at me.

'What happened?' I asked.

'Seriously?' she asked.

'What?'

'Do you think it matters where we end up finding peace for ourselves? Regardless of the place being a mosque or a church?'

'Uh, well . . .' I searched for the right words.

'I didn't expect you to follow such fundamental beliefs.'

I fell silent.

'Rehaan, we should not view it through a religious prism. As far as I know, peace is a subject common to all religions. Isn't that so?'

'Yeah, I guess,' I said and ran my fingers through my hair.

'I find peace here,' she said, gesturing towards the church building. 'But that doesn't make me any less of a Muslim. Where do you find your peace?'

I looked at her, furrowing my brows, without answering her.

'Is there any place where you find peace? Or any person you find peace with?' She looked at me.

I couldn't turn my gaze away from her, but I also didn't have an answer to her question. I remained quiet, continuing to stare at her.

'You're impossible. You know that? Come, let's go inside,' she said and took me by my arm, leading me into the building.

The church had a quaint look and a quiet ambience. We walked down the aisle till she stopped and ushered me to one of the benches, asking me to close my eyes. I waited to see what she did. She closed her eyes and started to pray. It was the first time I'd seen her praying. She looked a vision of serenity—seated at the bench, her eyes closed—and I felt I could almost hear her pray. I felt a little lost and didn't know what to do. If I closed my eyes to pray, I'd miss the chance to watch her from close while she was in a spiritual moment. She looked beautiful. If she had asked me then whom I found peace with, I would have an answer for her. I would have told her I found peace with her. I wish I had told her when she asked me outside the church. The moment I realized that she was about to open her eyes, I shut mine and pretended to pray.

The Unexpected

A few days later, I was out with Zynah for lunch at one of her favourite restaurants.

'How's the food?' Zynah asked me as she took a bite from her naan-e-barbari, one of the signature dishes made by the restaurant.

'It's good. It's different,' I nodded and said.

'I told you so,' she said, smiling at me.

'Is there any place you haven't taken me to yet?'

'Oh, c'mon. There are loads of places that I'd like you to visit. There is still a lot of London for you to see.'

'I am sure of that.'

Most of the time, when we were out for lunch or dinner, I never let Zynah pay. She insisted but I would not have it. I knew I was overstepping my budget but my part-time job helped me manage.

'So, you enjoyed the food?' she asked me after lunch.

'Yeah, the food was good, but, honestly, I felt the place was a bit boring,' I replied, amazed at my audacity.

'No doubt it is. Hey, Rehaan!' She stopped midway, looking at me.

I glanced at her sideways, raising a brow.

'Wanna have some real fun?' she asked me in an excited tone.

I looked at her, surprised, wondering what she was up to.

'Fun?' I asked her.

'Yes, real fun!' she said, with a wink.

Zynah's idea of 'real fun' was a trip to a nightclub. Yes, a nightclub. I couldn't imagine myself ever going to a nightclub, let alone with Zynah. For a moment, I was judgmental about Zynah. How often did she go to nightclubs? Was it routine for her or did she only want to show me the club? Zynah said that the club, The Nest, had recently opened but was the place to be. So it was always packed with clubbers. The atmosphere inside gave me a rush—the main hall was dimly lit except for the flashing strobe lights. People of all ethnicities were on the dance floor, their bodies swaying to the rhythm of the beat. The bar area was packed with people keeping the bartenders busy with unending orders of alcohol and fizzy drinks. Every corner of the club buzzed with energy.

'I see that you really like the place,' Zynah shouted in my ears, bringing me back from my reverie.

'No!' I blurted. 'I was just . . . you know, checking out . . .'.

'Checking out the hot girls?' she completed my sentence before I could and nudged my arm playfully, placing a cigarette between her lips.

My face flushed with embarrassment.

'No, not girls. I meant the place,' I said. I could feel my cheeks on fire.

'I wouldn't mind if you checked out the girls,' she said, patting me on my shoulder. 'Come, let's get drinks.'

'Okay,' I said, following her towards the bar.

We made it to the bar counter after wading through the crowd of drunk people, many of whom we bun.ped into.

'What would you like to have?' Zynah shouted over the deafening music from the speakers.

'Um, a lime soda?'

'What? Are you serious?' Her face fell.

'Yeah, what's wrong?'

'You're going to have a lime soda in a nightclub?' Zynah said with a look of shock on her face.

I shrugged.

'I bet they don't even have lime soda on the menu here,' she said, rolling her eyes.

'Then, what . . . ?'

'Let me order for you.'

I did not know what she was going to order. I looked around the nightclub. Everyone seemed to be comfortable and were focused on only enjoying the night.

'Two tequila shots, please!' she told the bartender, beaming.

I had heard about tequila shots but I had never had a chance to try them. I had never been to a nightclub back in Lahore.

'Hey, are you stupid?' I hissed in her ear. 'We can't drink that.'

'Why not? Are you here for fun or not, Captain?' she asked.

'I am but . . .'

'Then relax and trust me. I won't let anything happen to you,' she said, smiling.

I looked into her eyes.

'You trust me, right?' she asked, bringing her face close to mine.

'Yes,' I whispered.

'Then relax and don't worry.'

'Okay,' I sighed, shifting my thoughts back to the tequila shots.

It was not that I had not tried a drink before that. Occasionally, Ahmed and I would sneak out of college and grab beers. But that's all I had ever tried. The beer didn't taste so bad and did not affect my consciousness. Tequila shots were probably another thing. I had no idea what they were going to do to me.

'Do not fret, Captain. I was quite excited when my friends brought me here to drink tequila shots for the first time,' she told me.

'You've tried this before?' I asked her.

'Yeah, we do hang out here once a month.'

'Hmm.'

No matter what she did, I loved her. None of her shortcomings could make me un-love her.

The bartender, a smile fixed on his face, placed our tequila shots on the counter. Zynah also asked him to put some salt and lemon slices on a plate.

'What's that for?' I asked, gesturing at the plate.

'Okay, here's how you drink the tequila. First, you need to lick some salt.'

'Why?' I frowned.

'The salt lessens the burning effect of the alcohol.'

'Oh.' I raised my brows. 'That happens?'

'Yes, it does. After that, you're going to down the shot immediately. Then, quickly bite into and suck a lemon slice. That will help to balance and enhance the flavour of the tequila. Gotcha?'

'Okay, it seems easy,' I said, feeling the thrill shoot through my spine.

'So, are you ready?' she asked, putting a hand over my shoulder.

'Hell, yeah!'

'Let's go!' She placed a lemon slice between her thumb and index finger, put a pinch of salt on the back of her hand and held the shot glass in her other hand. She licked the salt off her hand, chugged down the tequila shot and clamped her teeth down on the flesh of the lemon slice with a slight grimace. I tried to follow what she had done. The salt was fine but as soon as the tequila hit my tongue, a burning sensation coursed down my tongue, past my tonsils and all the way to my belly button. I bit on the lemon slice. She was right. It made the sharp taste of the tequila better.

'Whoa!' I took a step back and exclaimed.

'How was it?' Zynah asked, wiping her lips with the back of her hand.

'Whoa,' I said. A switch had turned on a buzz inside my head.

'Want to go for another one?'

I hesitated, but just for a moment, before I nodded.

'Yes!' I confirmed. 'Once again.'

After having a couple of tequila shots, the buzz in my head became more pronounced and I lost track of time. We drank, we sang, and then we hit the floor to dance. I couldn't remember if I had ever had this much fun in my life. This had to be the best night since I came to London. I was conscious but I was not—I was oblivious to everything and everyone around me except for what we were doing. I didn't know if Zynah also felt the same because it was finally she who dragged me from the nightclub. I was still high and hummed songs as we strolled down the lonely streets of London.

'Rehaan, you need to control yourself. Come, let's sit down for a while,' she said, pulling me off the road and sitting me down on the pavement. I blinked my eyes and rubbed them with my fingers. The street lights were swimming.

'Are you okay?' she asked me with a hint of worry in her tone and concern in her eyes.

'Yes, I'm okay,' I told her.

'Your condition tells me otherwise. I shouldn't have let you drink more than one tequila shot.'

'I'm fine, Zynah. I'm really fine. Please don't worry,' I reassured her.

'Okay.'

I couldn't feel any worry about being drunk—I was busy experiencing the million bolts of electricity shooting through my body while Zynah held my hand in hers. I stared down at our hands interlocked, then back at her face and smiled. She smiled back.

'You know, you asked me where I find my peace before we were about to enter the St. Pancras Old Church,' I said.

'Hmm?' she hummed quietly, avoiding my gaze.

'Here. With you,' I finally told her.

I waited to catch the reaction on her face but she didn't turn towards me. She stared at the road. I could make out that her eyes were not focused on anything in particular. I thought that perhaps she hadn't heard me. Now, I felt stupid blurting it out.

'Zynah,' I said, my voice croaky. 'Are you listening?'

'It's so easy to talk about your feelings to someone . . . I wish I had that courage too,' she said, looking away dreamily.

Her words made me think that perhaps she also felt the same way. Perhaps she wanted to say so.

'Of course, you can talk about it,' I encouraged her, holding her hand firmly.

Suddenly, I felt stronger. The high from the tequila ebbed.

'Okay, let's look at it this way. We can express our feelings about someone to them but what really scares me is the uncertainty of how they will respond. Will they reciprocate your love or reject it?' she said and looked at me with questioning eyes.

'The person who rejects you will be a fool, Zynah,' I told her. 'A really BIG fool.'

'How can you say that?' she asked me, her eyes gleaming.

'Because, you're a wonderful woman. You're . . . you're amazing,' I stuttered, unable to find the right words to describe what she meant to me. I was short of words to say all of the things I had thought I might someday say to her.

'Do you think he thinks the same of me?' she asked, her voice softening, her gaze still affixed on the horizon.

'Of course,' I responded abruptly and then the meaning of her words hit me.

Zynah had turned her face and was now looking at me. I stared back at her, the effects of the tequila had left my brain and a cloud of doubt hung low.

'He?' I asked, perplexed. 'Who's he?'

Did she mean me? Maybe she was incoherent right now.

'Oh . . . damn . . .' she said and clamped her hands over her mouth, her eyes widening.

'What happened?' I asked, concerned.

The cloud of doubt had travelled down from over my head and was now a storm of fear in my heart. I felt an ache but I could not focus on it. I had to know what she meant.

'I'm sorry I haven't told you about him all this while . . .' she whispered, her voice slowly sinking away.

'About whom, Zynah?' I asked. The pain in my chest had become duller..

'About Aariz!' she blurted out finally.

The words stabbed into my heart.

'Aariz?' I asked her, and gulped.

'Yeah, Aariz. Aariz Kamran. My boss, the managing director of FK Designs, son of my dad's close friend and the person I am in love with.'

Nobody else heard the loud explosion that followed. My heart burst into tiny shards that seared the dull pain across my entire chest. No one saw the damage except for me. My whole body became numb. My eyes became watery. The saliva burned in my throat—more than the tequila had.

'Damn . . . I should have told you about him a long time ago!' she said.

I saw her elbow nudge me but I did not feel it. I could no longer feel any sensations.

'So, here's what happened . . .' she said, without waiting for me to respond. 'I finished college and was bored to death. Daddy wanted me to join his friend's firm. At first, I rejected the idea but when he told me that it was an interior design company, I decided to go for it. So, I joined the company as an intern last year and was later absorbed as an assistant designer. That's where I met Aariz.'

I looked down at my hands. I didn't know if I had heard her story properly. Everything around me seemed hazy.

'It seems he wasn't supposed to work in his dad's firm but since he was the only son, he had to take over. He moved from Canada to London and took over the firm. I met Aariz briefly at a party hosted by his father to introduce him and that's where I lost my heart to him. You know? Love at first sight . . .'

I winced when I heard that.

'I never believed in love at first sight but Aariz changed me. Everything about him is so magical, I can't even begin to tell you! He has a charismatic personality. He's so sophisticated, talented and decent. There's not a single girl in our office who hasn't had a crush on him,' she said, smiling to herself. 'He's the kind of person even men would like to be with.' She laughed and said, 'I'm sure you'll like him too!'

'Does he know that you . . . that you like him too?' I managed to ask, my voice cracking up.

Why couldn't she see how hurt I was? Had she even heard or understood the meaning of what I had said before she launched into describing her feelings for Aariz?

'Well, I am sure he knows. Our families know what I feel for him. Daddy, Mummy, Uncle Kamran and Aunty Raima, everyone knows. In fact, Uncle Kamran, Aariz's father, has also asked him to marry me.'

'What?' I could not believe my ears.

'Don't worry,' she said and let out a laugh. 'I'm not getting married right away. He hasn't agreed yet. He wants to take some time before making the decision. But, deep down, I know he likes me. And, I'm sure he's going to agree very soon.' She giggled.

I turned my face away; tears were now flowing down my cheeks.

The Loss

It was hard for me to cope with the reality of the heartbreak. I had somewhat endured the pain of Zynah leaving me when she had moved from Lahore to London a few years back but I had no idea how I was supposed to deal with this now. I wish I'd downed a few more tequila shots to forget whatever she said to me that night. Bearing the loss a second time around wouldn't be easy for me. Had Zynah only said that she liked someone, it may have been easier. But Zynah did not only like him, she was keen to marry him. She wanted to start a life with him. It was not a schoolgirl crush. She was serious about Aariz and being with him. After she told me her story, initially I thought that she might not be serious because she was drunk that night. But I was wrong.

The next morning I woke up to her call, and she asked me if I was hung-over from the night before. She apologized for making me drink too much. I lied and told her that I was fine. The conversation went smoothly for a while till she mentioned Aariz again. She apologized that she had not told me about him earlier. I had not met him yet but I felt hatred upon hearing his name. I wished that the night before had been an ugly dream. I wished I had woken up the next day and everything turned back to the way it was before. But it was real and realities do not change at whim. You have to accept them. Aariz was still very much there. Zynah was still serious about him. After I heard her apologize for not telling me about him, I changed the topic and lied to her that I was getting late for class. She told me that she wanted to meet me but I ignored her. I managed to end the call.

I got up from the bed and rushed into the washroom. As I splashed water on to my face, I realized what I had got myself into. Did I really come to London for love and heartbreaks? To deal with a messy love life? I had come here to study, to become independent and earn well enough to provide for my family. As my own reality hit me, I sat down on the toilet seat and thought about the direction my life was taking. I had deviated from my purpose because of Zynah. She had broken my heart back in high school but I would not let her do it again. I would face this heartbreak and fight it.

The Ignorance

A week had passed since the night Zynah had taken me to the nightclub and since she had told me about Aariz. I hadn't taken her phone calls since then nor had I replied to her text messages. I had many reasons to ignore her: She had broken my heart, yet again. I was angry at her and I wanted to tell her that. But, I was angrier at her for not being able to comprehend my feelings, for ignoring them when I had almost poured my heart out to her. Was that not what had set her off on a rant about her feelings for Aariz? Whenever I had met her earlier, it was always evident on my face how much I loved her. My final exams were fast approaching and I could not afford to give heed to these thoughts, the turmoil and the pain.

I promised myself that I would not break down. I wanted to stay strong and stick to the purpose I'd come here for. When she finally realized I'd been ignoring her, Zynah drove to my place one night. She sent me a text message after arriving below my residence and asked me to come outside. I cursed myself for having given her my address. The night was freezing cold and I was only dressed in a loose cardigan and pyjamas. She seemed amused by my appearance. I frowned at her.

'What's wrong?' I asked her, my brows furrowing.

I was seeing her after a week and it felt soothing. I had missed her. At the same time, the wound was still fresh. She stopped laughing after she heard me and her face became serious.

'What's wrong with me?' she asked. 'Dude, what's wrong with you? Why haven't you been receiving my calls?'

'I have my finals. I told you over the phone,' I said and looked away.

'Couldn't you even bother to reply to my texts? Are you that busy, nerdy?' she asked in a teasing tone.

'I told you I was busy with my exams, Zynah. Don't you get it?' I asked her sternly.

'Go fuck your exams then, Captain,' she cursed me, hopped back into her car and drove away.

I stood in the freezing cold, my jaw hanging in shock.

The next day, I decided to give Zynah a call. She cut my calls initially but accepted one after a few more attempts.

'What do you want?' she asked curtly.

'I want to talk to you. In fact, I want to meet you.'

'Fine. Today 5 p.m. Music store,' Click. She had hung up the phone.

I finished my work at the convenience store and took the Tube to meet her. At the music store, Zynah was in one of the aisles, large pink headphones astride her head.

'Hi,' I said to her with a wave and a smile.

'Hi,' she paused chewing her gum and returned my greeting with what was clearly a fake smile.

'Uh, what's up?' I asked, walking closer to her.

'Nothing. You had to say something?' she asked, changing the topic.

'Look,' I said with a sigh. 'You don't have to act so uptight, okay? Everything's cool.'

'Am I acting uptight? Oh, really?' she took off her headphones and put them down on the counter. 'Who was acting uptight last night?' she said, crossing her arms, waiting for me to respond.

'I know I acted like a jerk. I shouldn't have done that. I'm sorry.'

'Oh, right. So you're sorry now,' she said, rolling her eyes.

'Yeah, I am,' I said, and raised my arms up in the air in mock surrender.

'You really want me to forgive you?' she asked, raising a brow.

'Yes!'

'Cool. But, you have to work for it.'

'Work? What work?' I asked.

'Come with me.'

Had I known that all she needed was a scoop of ice cream to forgive me, I would have come armed with some. I got her a two-scoop cup of Ben & Jerry's chocolate fudge brownie flavour from the store next door and she quickly grabbed it from my hands. I looked at her while she ate her ice cream. I wished she knew how much I cared for her and loved her...

As we walked to the closest Tube station, she began to talk.

'You know, I really think I should have told you about Aariz much earlier,' she said, looking down.

The mention of his name annoyed me but I didn't show it when I turned to look at her.

'We have been friends for a long time but I never brought up his name in front of you. I'm sorry. I know it's my fault. I was behaving like a happy-go-lucky person all this while. I didn't care about the world, but look at me now. What a sick, lovelorn girl I have become,' she said with a nervous giggle.

I looked down, hiding the discomfort in my eyes.

'You know, I've known him for only a few months and it already seems like a lifetime,' she said, sighing, with a lost expression on her face.

'Zynah?' I asked, looking at her.

'Hmm?'

'Do you really love him?'

She stopped midway and turned to look at me. I stopped and looked at her too. Her eyes didn't say anything. I wish I could understand what was going on in her head but her face betrayed nothing. After a few seconds, she slowly nodded at me and then resumed walking.

'Why?' I asked her, to which she stopped again.

'What kind of a question is that?' she snorted as she turned around to look back at me.

'It's a simple question. Why do you think you love him?'

'There's nothing about Aariz that can stop someone from loving him. He's everything a man should be. He's extremely handsome, affluent, well-settled in a career, sophisticated and comes from a decent family. He's got everything a girl desires.'

'Is that all?' I asked, quite surprised at her typical girlish response.

'Of course! What else could there be?'

'No, actually, I was thinking . . . what if you merely have a crush on him? What if it is just an infatuation? Perhaps you're confusing attraction with love.'

Her expression grew serious.

'Rehaan, I'm not a child. I would have known if I merely had a crush on him but I don't. So, stop doubting my feelings for him,' she snapped back and then started to walk again.

I quickened my pace to match her steps.

'All right, all right. I'm sorry. I know now that you love him but what about him? Does he love you the way you do?'

'Of course, he does!' she said. I could sense the annoyance in her tone.

'Has he ever told you?' I grilled her even more.

'No, he hasn't but he will!'

'How can you be so sure of that?' I asked. 'What if he never does? What if you're living an illusion? What if he doesn't love you?'

'Shut up, Rehaan. It's nothing like that!'

'Maybe it is, Zynah. That's why he hasn't agreed to marry you.'

She stopped once again and looked at me, her face dead serious.

'What fool would delay in marrying you, huh? Tell me,' I asked her in a demanding tone.

'Stop it, Rehaan. Just stop it! What's your problem? Why are you acting like a fucktard since the moment I told you about Aariz?' she asked, fuming.

I looked around, anger filling every cell of my body.

'Maybe you're jealous!' she snapped.

'What? Why would I be jealous of him?' I was shocked.

'Because Aariz has everything and you don't!'

'What the hell are you saying? I don't give a damn about what he has.'

'That's good, now, listen to me,' she said, pointing a finger at me. 'I don't want to hear anything else from you on this topic, regarding him. Do you understand?'

'Fine, even I don't want to talk about him,' I mumbled, running my fingers through my hair. I couldn't believe what she had just said. Did she really love him for these superficial reasons?

'I am going home. I don't think I want to be with you right now. Bye,' she said, taking faster strides towards the Tube station.

The Inevitable

It had been a few weeks since Zynah and I had spoken to each other. I had got busy preparing for my midterms and then had spent extra hours at the store. I would be lying if I said I hadn't missed Zynah. I would check my phone often, hoping to receive a call or message from her. But that never happened. My three-week semester break had begun and I was trying hard to keep myself busy and not think about her.

I looked at the clock as it struck 11 p.m. It was a Saturday evening but I was still at the store, working a double shift. I sauntered out around midnight and slowly made my way towards the apartment. As I stepped on to the porch, I saw Vikram and Avantika exiting the front door.

'Hey dude, what's up?' Vikram asked, shutting the door behind him.

'Nothing, just tired. Had a double shift today,' I said, climbing up the stairs.

'Tired already? It's Saturday night!' Vikram exclaimed. 'We're going to the pub down the road. Do you want to come along for a few drinks?'

I narrowed my eyes, thinking what to do. I had had a long day and was allowed a little fun, so I said yes.

We drove to the pub in Vikram's car. Vikram and Avantika got busy with their friends as soon we entered, leaving me alone. I walked towards the bar to get myself a drink. A blonde wearing a short electric-blue dress was perched atop a bar stool, her gaze fixed on me. She smiled at me coquettishly and beckoned me to join her.

She asked me to buy her a drink, so I ordered a tequila shot for her. When she realized I hadn't ordered anything for myself, she called the bartender and ordered one for me as well.

She winked at me before downing her drink and then ordered another round. I took a deep breath and gulped mine too, one after the other. She ordered another round and then another. I soon lost track and drained shot after shot. She then held my hand and led me to the dance floor. She put her arms around my neck and started swaying to the music. I tried to match her steps but was reminded of Zynah and our night together. Her face flashed in front of my eyes. I felt dizzy and the music felt uncomfortably loud. The darkness closed in on me and I felt trapped in the girl's arms. I moved away from her as a wave of claustrophobia hit me. I ran out of the club in a panic, my heart thudding in my chest. I leaned against a wall and tried to get my bearings. I folded my arms against the biting wind and walked unsteadily in the direction of my apartment. I couldn't see where I was going and before I knew it, I was in the middle of the road. Headlights from a speeding car blinded me and I

covered my face with my arm. I waited and waited until
I heard a loud bang.

🎧

After a few hours, I woke up in my bedroom. My body
ached. My head hurt. I sat up and checked the time on
my cell phone—it was 2 a.m.

'Rehaan, how are you feeling now?' Avantika peeped
into the room, holding a mug in her hands. Vikram stood
behind her.

'Yeah, I feel better,' I said, dragging myself out of the
bed.

'Why did you drink so much if you knew you
wouldn't be able to handle it?' Avantika asked as she sat
next to me.

'I don't know . . . I don't remember anything. How
did I . . . end up here?'

'We found you walking in the middle of the road.
Vikram saved you in the nick of time.'

I looked at Vikram and he nodded reassuringly.

'We brought you home and splashed water on your
face, but you wouldn't wake up. You kept asking for
Zynah in your sleep.'

My face crimsoned on hearing this.

'What? Did I really say her name?' I asked,
embarrassed.

'You are in love with this girl, huh?' Vikram teased
me.

'We were so worried and decided to call Zynah here.
It seemed like the reasonable thing to do.'

'Wait, what did you do?' My heart thumped loudly
in my chest.

'We got Zynah's number from your phone and called her. Simple,' Vikram said.

'What?' I stood up, feeling a rush of adrenaline. 'Why would you guys do that?' I scowled.

'Because we didn't have an option.'

'Damn,' I hissed.

'She is on her way,' Avantika said. 'You'd better have a cup of coffee before she comes.'

'No! I am absolutely fine, just tell me, why did you call her?'

'Well, you just woke up. You were in a really bad state an hour ago. You should thank us for not contacting your family members.'

'Damn, damn, damn . . .' I said, pacing the room.

'Wait, I think she's already here. I heard a car pull up in the driveway,' Vikram said and left the room.

I cursed them under my breath.

Zynah was waiting for me outside the house. I put on a navy-blue cardigan and went out to meet her. She seemed angry. I couldn't bring myself to look at her.

'Zynah . . .' I mumbled as I approached her.

'What the hell is wrong with you, Captain? You want to get yourself killed?' she asked, her face red with anger.

'Zynah . . .'

'Don't touch me!' she screamed. 'What do you think you're doing? Huh? What's your problem? Are you depressed? Are you out of your mind? What is wrong with you, Rehaan? What is it?'

'You!' I yelled. 'You are my problem, Zynah. You!' I said, raising my finger.

Her expression changed from anger to shock. My words brought colour to her face and she looked away.

'What?' she whispered. 'What do . . . you . . . mean?'

'In fact,' I said, 'I never got over you, Zynah. Not even when you left Pakistan.'

She looked at me, half astonished, half confused.

'That's true, Zynah. I have had feelings for you since we were in school and I . . . I can't bear the thought of you being with someone else. I can't see you with anyone else other than me,' I said, and stepped closer, my hands around her shoulders.

She looked into my eyes, shocked.

'I love you, Zynah. I've . . . always loved you,' I whispered, my grip tightening.

'Rehaan . . .' she whispered, shaking her head in disbelief.

'It was love at first sight. Now you tell me . . . Who deserves you more? Me or that guy who doesn't even give a shit about you?'

'Rehaan, listen to me . . .' she said, fidgeting with her scarf.

'Who deserves your love? Me or him?' I asked again.

'Rehaan . . . you're not in your senses . . .'

'Who deserves to be with you, Zynah? Who deserves to see you, to feel you, to touch you . . .?' I said, leaning closer and planting a kiss on her lips.

'Stop it, Rehaan! What the hell are you doing?' she screamed and pushed me forcefully.

I just stood there, my head hung low in shame.

'We are friends, Rehaan, for God's sake!' her voice softened as she took a step towards me. 'What's wrong with you? God . . . come here . . .' she said and held me in an embrace.

I embraced her back, forgetting everything around us. I took in her fragrance and buried my face in her hair. She ran her hand through my hair and tried to calm me down. But nothing felt right. There was a storm brewing inside me.

'Rehaan, what we feel for each other is love . . . I understand that. But we love each other as friends. It's nothing more than that . . . You need to understand that,' she whispered.

I kept quiet as I didn't agree with her. What I felt was love; it was more than friendship.

'I love you, Rehaan, but only as a friend . . . I have feelings for someone else. I love Aariz . . .'

I pulled away and looked at her in bewilderment.

'Rehaan, listen to me . . .' she said, reaching for my hand, but I shook her off.

'No!' I raised my hand, interrupting her. 'You don't understand me, Zynah. This is not friendship. This is love. I love you, Zynah. With all my heart and soul.'

'Please stop it, Rehaan,' she said, closing her eyes.

'Believe me . . . for once,' I pleaded, my eyes boring into hers.

'I can't take this any more. I'm leaving,' she said and ran back to her car. I realized I was losing her. Or perhaps I'd already lost her. I rushed towards her and banged on her car window.

'You need to go back inside. Take some rest. You're not thinking clearly,' she told me as she rolled down the window.

'Zynah, listen to me . . . Understand what I'm saying. He is just not right for you.'

'Shut the hell up, Rehaan. You can't decide who is right or wrong for me. Just mind your own fucking business!' she said, her eyes filled with hatred.

'I don't want to see you ever again!' she said and revved the engine.

I moved away, my body shaking with rage. 'I wish he dies, Zynah. I wish your Aariz dies!' I screamed at the top of my voice.

She stopped her car and jutted her head out to look at me.

'I wish he cheats on you. I wish he rejects you. I wish he turns out to be a criminal. I wish he turns out to be gay!' I yelled.

Vikram and Avantika came running out of the house when they realized what was happening.

Zynah looked at me in shock, her eyes filled with tears.

'Come inside, Rehaan. I think you're done here!' Vikram said and grabbed me by my arm, dragging me inside the house.

The Misery

When I was not working, I spent most of my free time in bed. I rarely spoke to anyone back home. I crawled into bed as soon as I got home from work, ignoring Vikram and Avantika. I did not even step downstairs apart from getting something to eat. Both Vikram and Avantika tried to talk sense into me but I did not listen.

I had lost all contact with Zynah. She had said she would never see me again let alone talk to me. I had also promised myself not to see her ever. She chose someone else. She chose to ignore my feelings. So I chose to forget her. I realized it was for the best. When I did not answer calls from home for some days, it worried my family members, who sensed that something was wrong. Shaidi Mamu managed to get hold of Vikram's phone number from Rahim Uncle and called Vikram on his phone. Vikram told him what I was going through and how I was dealing with the heartbreak. Shaidi Mamu told Amma about the course my love story had taken. She called Vikram and requested him to get me to talk to her.

'What the hell?' I asked Vikram when he thrust the phone on to my ear.

'You have a call from home,' he said.

'What?' I said, shocked. Vikram pulled his hand away, and I managed to catch the phone just before it fell.

'Talk, please,' Vikram said and walked into the kitchenette.

'Wait, what did you tell them?' I called after him, putting a hand over the speaker.

'Whatever they have a right to know!' Vikram shouted back.

I panicked. So, my family now knew what I was going through. Vikram had told them everything. About me. About Zynah. About my heartbreak. I took a deep breath, gathering the courage to speak to them.

'Hello?' I said.

'Rehaan! Beta, are you all right? Where have you been?' Amma asked in a worried tone.

'I'm fine, Amma. Don't worry. Everything's fine here.'

'What is this that we have heard about you? What are you up to in London?'

'Amma . . . Nothing,' I stammered.

'Are you involved with some girl?' she asked.

I was scared and did not know how to respond. Had I told them the truth, my family would have been disappointed in me.

'No, Amma. There's no girl. I was just feeling sick and I'm fine now. You know how life here is. It is tough. I was stressed out because of the exams but I'm doing much better now.'

'Is some girl troubling you? Tell me, Rehaan. Vikram has told us everything,' she persisted.

'There's nothing to tell.' I kept up the lie. 'Please trust me.'

'But beta, we are worried for you.'

'Amma, I said I'm fine. Please don't worry.'

'Are you sure?'

'Yes.'

'Acha, beta, please answer our calls, okay?'

'Okay, I will.'

'Acha, now talk to Azaan. He is eager to talk to you.'

Amma passed the phone to Azaan, Abba and then Shaidi Mamu. All of them seemed concerned for me and complained that I had been out of touch for too long. I wondered if I'd really created a mess for myself. After I was done with the phone call, I looked for Vikram to return his phone but he was nowhere to be found. I headed upstairs and before I could knock on his door, Avantika opened it from inside, clad in a nightdress. I hesitated briefly before looking up at her and then handed her Vikram's phone. As I turned to walk away, she held me by my hand.

'You wanna talk?' she asked.

She brewed coffee for the both of us while I waited on the couch in the TV lounge. A football match played on the TV in the background but I wasn't watching it.

'Here you go,' she said and handed me a cup of coffee.

'Thanks, Avantika,' I told her.

'Do you know how Vikram and I met?' she asked. 'We met in college four years ago.'

I put down my cup on the coffee table.

'We did not like each other at first. Whenever he was close, I used to run away,' she said with a laugh. 'But then, one day, when I saved him from getting expelled, we became friends and that's how it began.'

I smiled at her.

'His parents were against our relationship. They still are. But Vikram is adamant on being with me.'

'But why are they against your relationship?' I asked, curious.

'Because I don't match up to their expectations. I belong to a middle-class family and his family is much richer than mine,' she said, rolling her eyes. 'His family thinks I am a gold-digger, out to trap their son for money.'

I considered her response, slowly nodding.

'Vikram says true love fights against all odds. The day his parents realize that his happiness lies with me, and only me, they'll stop opposing our love and accept us.'

I stirred the coffee in my cup, the difficulty of their relationship sinking in.

'Perhaps there is a lesson in there for you, Rehaan,' Avantika said, putting her hand over mine. 'You should also realize that maybe Zynah is happy with someone else. If you love her, you should prioritize her happiness.'

I looked at her, confused as hell.

'Learn to be happy for her. Find your happiness in hers and move on.'

Tears welled up in my eyes, but I tried not to blink.

'Do not ruin your friendship with her. It is precious, sacred. Appreciate it and never let it go.'

I wiped my tears and nodded at her.

'Go and talk to her. Make up with her.'

She clasped my hand firmly.

I nodded; the firmness of her grip helped me gather my resolve.

'Thank you, Avantika. Thank you.' I held her hand back and pressed it firmly.

🎧

I changed my clothes in a jiffy and booked an Uber. On my way, I kept trying to reach Zynah but her number was not reachable. Whatever Avantika had told me made sense. Why hadn't I thought of it that way? I had ruined my friendship with Zynah because I wanted to create a new relationship with her. How could I forge a new relationship with her if its foundation—our friendship—had become weak? I had made her hate me. I had said inappropriate things to her. I did not know if she'd ever listen to me or forgive me but I had to try and apologize to her for my immature behaviour. I had to convince her that I couldn't lose our friendship. That's all I had. It had been a month since I had seen her last and I couldn't wait to see her face again.

I got off the taxi at Willow Road, rushed to her door and banged hard. A short, elderly woman with plump cheeks opened the door for me. I realized this was Zynah's mother.

'Yes?' she asked.

'Salaam, Aunty. I'm Rehaan. I'm Zynah's friend.'

'Ohhh. You're Rehaan! Zynah has spoken a lot about you!' she said and patted me on my shoulder. I tried to look around for Zynah but there were no signs of her.

'I'm happy to meet you finally,' she said, smiling.

'Me too, Aunty. Is Zynah here?'

'Why weren't you at the wedding?' she asked, interrupting me.

Her words felt like a punch in the face.

'Wedding?' I said, choking back tears.

'Yes, Zynah's wedding ceremony last week. Why weren't you there? All of her friends were there, except you.'

A buzz in my ears muted the rest of her words. Someone had hit pause and time seemed to have come to a standstill. My heart sank because I realized I'd lost Zynah as a friend too.

Present Day

Tears formed a pool at the edge of my eyelids. Something had brought back the memories from the night Zynah's mother told me of her wedding. Other flashbacks followed and I did not realize that we had reached her location. I slowed down the car as we neared the place where the support group met. I did not know why she was going there. I saw her in the rear-view mirror as she wiped her tears, tucked her hair behind her ears and sniffed. She placed a ten-pound note next to her on the back seat, opened the door and stepped outside, without looking back at me. She had not even bothered to ask me the fare. I was too bewildered to react. However, I did not want to end this chance meeting. I disembarked quickly and followed her to the main entrance of the support group centre. I walked through the glass door, scanning the place. A small group of people had gathered in the main hall, sitting on chairs set in a circle. Zynah was sitting on one of the chairs, her expression blank.

Why is she here? I thought.

I slowly tiptoed towards the hall when someone tapped on my shoulder.

'Excuse me, sir?' said a young lady, perhaps in her early twenties. 'Have you registered to attend this session?'

At first, I thought of concocting a story but decided against it since I might land in trouble. This was London and I could not afford to be kicked out for fooling around.

'No, I'm not. But I would like to register for it,' I told her, nodding.

'I'm sorry, sir, but the registrations have closed. You can join another session next week.'

Damn. Why? I thought.

'All right, but can you please tell me what this session is for?' I asked her.

'Today's session is to discuss anxiety and depression and how to fight against it,' she told me in a mechanical voice.

I weighed her response and turned around to look at Zynah sitting in the circle.

Why was she depressed or anxious? I thought.

Heading back towards the parking lot, I decided to wait for her until she came out.

Leaning against my car, I kept my eyes on the glass door at the entrance. I could have spoken to her when she was in the car but her sadness had stopped me. Soon afterwards, Zynah came out, looking at her cell phone. Was she booking a ride through the Uber app? Afraid that she might book another car instead of mine, I hurried over to her.

'Need a ride?' I asked, huffing. I was standing only a few inches from her.

She looked at me briefly when she heard my voice and turned to look back at her phone screen. After a few seconds, she looked at me again, squinting her eyes.

'Rehaan?' she asked; her eyes widened when she recognized me.

I nodded at her exuberantly as tears pricked my eyes. It had been a long time since I had seen her, let alone from this close. Her eyes were sunk, her cheeks hollow. I could barely see the thin layer of make-up on her face.

'Oh my God . . .' she gasped. 'It's been so long'

'Three years,' I told her, my eyes not leaving hers.

'Yes, it's been three years,' she agreed.

'We . . . uh . . . actually met two hours ago . . . in my car back there,' I signalled towards my car parked on the sideway as she followed my stare.

'What?' she said, looking confused.

'I drove you here. I drive part-time, mostly on weekends.'

'Really? I didn't know you'd take the nickname 'Captain' so seriously!' she said, her eyes showing surprise.

I was glad there was no tension between us after so long, given our tumultuous parting.

'Well, you can tease me later but let me tell you that I also happen to own a photography studio, if that makes you feel any better,' I told her, grinning.

'That's great,' she said, her astonishment giving way to a smile.

But the smile seemed superfluous. It seemed as if she was trying hard to look happy for me.

'So, how's life? How are you holding up?' I asked, folding my arms across my chest, steering the topic to another direction.

'Life is good. Everything is good,' she said and nodded, clutching her handbag tightly.

'And . . . what are you doing here?' I gestured towards the support centre.

'Oh, this?' she asked nervously

'*Pagal toh nahin hogayi sach mein*? [I hope you have not actually gone mad?]' I said, stifling a laugh.

She shot me a look of anger before her lips twitched into a smile.

'Just kidding!' I told her, throwing my hands up in the air. 'Actually, I had never expected to come across you all of a sudden. I'm so glad to see you after a long time, Zynah.'

'Me too,' she said slowly.

'Should I drop you home?' I asked, reading her face.

'Um, no thanks. I've asked a friend to pick me up from the market across the road. I guess I should leave,' she said and moved past me.

'Yeah but . . .'

'It was lovely seeing you, Rehaan. Take care. Bye,' she said, closing the conversation abruptly. She walked away. My gaze followed her until she disappeared into one of the shops across the street.

My eyes fell on a card lying face down on the ground just a few inches away from my feet, where she had stood earlier. It was Zynah's membership card for the support group; her initials were written on it. I shoved the card into my pocket, deciding I would drop it at her place the next day. This way I'd also get a chance to meet her parents and ask them if everything was okay in their daughter's life. Though I had no right to interfere in her life, I felt I wanted to know how she was.

🎧

As planned, the next morning I went to drop Zynah's card at her house on Willow Road in Hampstead. I thought her parents still lived there. Parking the car in the driveway, I got out and looked around. Everything looked the same. Mr Malik opened the door for me when I rang the bell.

'Yes?' he asked, furrowing his brows.

Even after a gap of three years, he still looked the same, sturdy and charming.

'Good afternoon, Malik Uncle. Did you not recognize me?' I asked, smiling.

He studied my face for a few seconds before his face broke into a smile.

'Oh! Rehaan! How are you, beta?' he said and embraced me in a tight hug. The embrace made me realize that I had missed these people in my life.

'I'm good, Uncle. How about you?'

'Come inside.'

As he ushered me in, a wave of nostalgia hit me and brought back numerous memories—some endearing, some nasty.

'We thought you had returned to Pakistan.'

The word 'we' made me wonder if it included Zynah.

'I do visit Pakistan once a year but I am based in London for now,' I told him as we made our way to the TV lounge.

He asked me what I was doing in London for a living and I told him about running a photography studio and driving for Uber on weekends. He appreciated my efforts by saying he was proud of me. He offered me tea but I politely refused.

'So, what brings you here today, young man?'

'I, uh, actually met Zynah last night outside a support group centre,' I said, fishing the card out of my pocket. 'It fell out of her handbag so I came here to return it.' I placed the card on the coffee table.

He picked up the card with shaking fingers and looked at it.

Noticing the oddness in his behaviour, I decided to ask him about her.

'Uncle, is . . . is Zynah doing okay?' I stammered.

'What do you mean, beta?' he asked in a low voice.

'What I mean is, she's a part of a support group . . . people join such groups only when they're facing some problems. So, I wanted to know if she is okay . . .'

'She is fine. Yes, we did ask her why she had joined this group. She said she had joined it for her own peace of mind and satisfaction. At least that's what she told us,' he said, shrugging his shoulders.

I pursed my lips and nodded at him.

'Her husband, Aariz, is a nice guy. She seems happy with him,' he said but it seemed as if he was trying to convince himself.

My heart cringed at hearing his name. I couldn't forget him. He had taken away my happiness.

'I hope she is,' I said, nodding. 'I should take your leave now, Uncle.' I stood up and shook hands with him.

'It was good to meet you after a long time. Do visit when your aunt is at home. She's out for a routine medical check-up.'

'How is she doing now?' I asked, suddenly remembering the panic attacks she used to have.

'She's fine. More stable than before,' he said.

'Take care of yourself, Uncle. I will see you around soon.'

On my way out, my eyes strayed to the wall covered with lots of framed photos. I zoomed in on one in which Zynah stood dressed as a bride with a man by her side. Their faces seemed happy. At that moment, I realized she had been right all along. Aariz definitely looked sophisticated, decent and like he had a charismatic personality. Perhaps I would look like a dunce in front of him.

🎧

Thankfully, I had to attend Vikram and Avantika's anniversary party that evening because thoughts about Zynah continued to occupy my mind. Her eyes, her smile, her face—everything about her had possessed me once again. I found myself under her spell yet again. She had joined a support group to get away from whatever issues she was facing and her family was okay with it. So, why should it worry me? I must not encroach upon her privacy. I went to the party to get away from these thoughts. I searched for the waiter across the bar to order a drink, but instead my eyes landed on someone else. Dressed in a button-down Hawaiian shirt and cream-coloured cotton pants, he was seated on a bar stool, smoking a cigarette and laughing with a bunch of people around him, all swaying lightly to the music. I tried to remember where I'd seen him before. One of the women with him gave a light peck on his cheek and he smiled at her.

Why did his face look so familiar?

It suddenly struck me. This was Zynah's husband, Aariz. I was positive that it was him. I couldn't forget the face from the wedding photo I had seen earlier that day. But, what was he doing amidst a bunch of women? The way he flirted with them and vice versa didn't seem proper. Was he having an affair behind Zynah's back? Was this the reason why Zynah had sought help from a support group? It started to make sense now.

Clenching my fists hard, I stepped quickly towards him but someone grabbed me midway.

'Rehaan! Where are you going?' I turned around to find Avantika glaring at me.

'Oh, hi,' I exhaled deeply.

'What's up? Are you okay?' she said with a look of suspicion.

'Yeah, I am perfectly okay. Were you looking for me?' I asked her, changing the subject.

'Yes! We're going to cut the cake on the top floor. Come, join us.'

She held my arm and dragged me away.

I turned around to take a quick look at the jerk who was still flirting with the women. I couldn't believe Zynah had left me for this prick. She chose *this man* over me. Why Zynah? *Why?*

🎧

The next morning, I dragged myself out of bed, my head throbbing from a hangover. Ruffling my hair, I made a

stop at the kitchen to switch on the espresso machine
for a shot of coffee. I sat down on a stool at the counter.
Flashbacks from last night ran through my head. I
wanted to tell Zynah everything I had witnessed at the
club. Whatever followed next was up to her. Whether
she considered me a friend or not, I knew I had to play
my part. Either she was too naive to notice anything or
she pretended to ignore it. Both of these options seemed
unlike her. Whatever she decided, I had to get this off
my chest. My cell phone buzzed, breaking my reverie. It
was a call from my assistant at the studio, Hassan.

'Yeah?' I asked.

'Morning! Are you done selecting the pictures? I kept
waiting for your email until late last night. I left a call and
a message but there was no response.'

'Shoot!' I hissed. I had completely forgotten that I
had work. 'Yeah, I have,' I lied to him as I sprinted to my
room to grab the laptop.

'I'll send the email to you in a second. Hold on.'
With the cell phone tucked under my ear, I got the laptop
and put it on the kitchen counter. The espresso machine
beeped. Damn! My coffee!

'No! Don't send them through email. Store them on
the USB drive,' Hassan said from the other end.

'USB drive?' I asked, ruffling my hair, confused.

'The one I left yesterday?' he reminded.

I looked for it, and found it still plugged into the
laptop.

'Yeah,' I said, detaching it from the laptop. 'I have it.'

'Great. I'll come over to get it.'

'Sure, I'm heading out in an hour so you won't find
me here. Ping me whenever you need me.'

'You going somewhere?'

'Yeah,' I said, my mind drifting back to Zynah. 'I have an important meeting to attend.'

It was drizzling when I jutted my head out of the car to take a quick peek at the main entrance of the support centre. I had taken a chance as I had no idea when she attended the sessions. Malik Uncle would have definitely told her that I dropped by her place to return her membership card.

Feeling the drops of rain on my face, I closed my eyes for a few seconds as I waited for her to appear. My intuition proved to be right. I opened my eyes to find her standing a few feet away from me, her arms folded.

Straightening myself, I motioned at her with a quick wave. There was no response from her. She didn't move when I took short steps towards her. When she saw me approach, she shook her head briskly and started to turn away.

'Zynah!' I called after her, almost sprinting. 'Wait!'

'Why are you following me, Rehaan?' she asked, twirling around, a few strands of her hair falling over her face. Her look was colder than the wind.

'I . . .' The words trailed away as I looked at her, my face solemn. 'I'm not following you, Zynah. I just wanted to . . .'

'Really?' She crossed her arms, cutting me in between. 'What were you doing yesterday at my place, then? Spying around? Asking my family if I was happy or not? What makes you so interested in my life all of a sudden?'

She took a jab at me and I stood there, clueless, my jaw hanging open.

'What?' I whispered, shocked. 'Didn't your dad tell you that I stopped by to drop off your card?'

'You could have also handed over the damn card to the help desk inside or given it to me directly,' she said, her accusing eyes piercing through me.

'I would suggest you keep a distance from me and my family. It will be better for the both of us.' She adjusted the handbag flung across her shoulder and prepared to walk away.

I could not comprehend what had made her so furious—asking her family about her or because she found me waiting for her now. Whatever the reason for her reaction, I decided not to stay quiet and watch her walk away.

'And I would suggest that you leave your flirt of a husband before he intends to hurt you even more.'

There, I had said it. Out loud. Finally.

I didn't want to regret my words but I did feel a slight pang of remorse. Luckily, my words had their effect. Zynah stopped in her tracks without turning towards me. I walked towards her, crossing where she stood until I stood face-to-face with her.

Zynah's eyes looked at the ground near her feet. She didn't flinch a muscle while I stood across her, waiting for her to react.

'Listen, Zynah, I did not mean to hurt you or . . .'

'What . . .what did you say about my husband?' she interrupted with a hiss. She finally looked up.

'Can we go and talk somewhere else, please?' I said with a pleading look.

🎧

Holding two cups of coffee in my hands, I made my way towards Zynah who was sitting in a café near the Tower Bridge which overlooked the river. Her eyes were set on the moving river. The skies had opened up and it was pouring again. I handed her the cup but she refused to take it with a gesture of her hand.

'Rehaan, I am not here for coffee. You were supposed to tell me something,' she said, her face turning serious again.

'Fine . . . ' I said, realizing she was here only to hear what I had to say. 'Let's come to the point. I saw your husband at the Egg Club last night, surrounded with goris. I am sure he was flirting with them. One of them was literally throwing herself on him.'

'And what makes you so sure that person was Aariz?' she asked, her voice laced with irritation. 'You've not even seen him!'

'I have!' I said. She furrowed her brows in confusion. 'I saw your wedding picture at your parents' place the other day,' I said slowly, a little embarrassed for being nosy.

Zynah shook her head.

'No, that person can't be Aariz. You're definitely mistaken. And I think I've wasted my time by coming here and listening to your lies.'

'Zynah, I'm not mistaken. I saw him. It was him. I swear!'

'You must have seen him at the club, but I don't believe the story about him flirting with other women,' she said, looking away.

'Zynah, trust me. That guy does not deserve you. He is seeing other women behind your back. He is cheating . on you!'

'He can't do that!' she screamed.

'Why not?' I screamed back.

'He just can't!' She turned her face away as tears rolled down her cheeks. It felt like she was hiding something from me.

She stood up and rushed out of the café. I followed her.

'Zynah, he can!' I shouted after her. 'Why would a loyal husband party with other women on a weekend night instead of spending time with his wife? Tell me, why?' I egged her on, holding her hand to make her stop.

'You don't know him, so stop it!' she said, shoving me away.

'And you know him? You can vouch for his loyalty?'

'Yes, I know him, dammit! He can't flirt with women,' she said, frowning agitatedly.

'What?' I looked at her in disbelief. 'I saw him with those women with my own eyes!'

'He is not into women!'

'What? Who is he into then?'

'He's into men!'

My jaw dropped when I heard her say those last four words. What did she mean? Had she made a mistake? She looked at me dejectedly. I took a step towards her and held her as she dropped her head, her shoulders slumped. I'd never seen her so vulnerable, so weak, so lifeless. Who was this person standing in front of me? Where was my old Zynah? What had Aariz turned her into? What had this marriage done to her?

'What are you saying, Zynah?' I asked, my lips trembling.

'He's into men . . .' she mumbled. 'My husband is gay,' she blurted.

PART THREE
Zynah

Where It All Began

London, UK

My life changed after I got married. I used to be the kind
of person who couldn't tolerate injustice or lies. I used to
speak up, voice my opinion. But I was a different person
now. The last three years had made me dispirited and
subdued.

After I finished college, my father suggested that I
join his friend's, Uncle Kamran's, interior design firm
but I refused. It was my dream job but I wasn't ready
to take on new responsibilities. I wanted to explore
the world, visit beautiful cities, meet new people, learn
new languages and have fun. There were days when I
just wanted to roam the streets of London, visiting my
favourite music stores and cafes. However, one night, one
meeting, or should I say one person made me question my
life choices—Aariz Kamran. Uncle Kamran had thrown
a party at his house in honour of his son, Aariz, who had
just returned from Canada to join his father's business.
I had met Uncle Kamran and his wife, Aunty Raima, at
a couple of dinners but had never met their son. I was

standing near the food counters, talking to someone, when he walked in. Our eyes locked briefly and in just that second, I lost my heart to him. His good looks were to be blamed. My eyes followed him as he walked to the other end of the room. I noticed how he brushed his hair back with his fingers every few seconds; how he threw his head back when he laughed; how keenly he listened, nodding ever so slightly in agreement. I studied him intently, tracing his lean body, his broad shoulders, his chiselled features, his taut jawline, his full lips, his slightly ruffled hair. I was new to these feelings—the flutter in my chest; the prickle of excitement; the quickening of pulse, and the wetness between my legs. That night I made up my mind to take Daddy up on his offer. It was the only way to be close to Aariz. I was ready to join FK Designs.

Crazy in Love

It did not take me long to fall head over heels for Aariz. I was amazed at how quickly I had developed feelings for this man. It wasn't entirely my fault—Aariz was irresistible. He was soft-spoken, decent and quite mature. I soon realized that I wasn't the only one who was smitten with his good looks. My other colleagues too nursed similar feelings for him. He was the subject of most of our lunch conversations, where they spoke highly of him and blushed whenever he addressed them. But I wasn't jealous because he flattered me with his attentions. Whenever he walked past our room, he made it a point to stop and talk to me for a few minutes. This, of course, made the other women envious. When they questioned me, I assured them that there was nothing between us and that we were only family friends, which was, in fact, true. They believed me at first but their suspicions were confirmed the day I was promoted to an assistant designer's post after completing the probation period. I decided to ignore their comments and focus on my work.

Aariz and I did meet outside office—we sometimes walked over to the nearby coffee shop for lunch or attended dinner parties at each other's homes with our families. The best part about these meetings was the conversations. We talked about everything—from discussing the most random things to giving voice to our goals and desires. He told me about his life in Canada—his house, his friends, their favourite haunts—and how much he missed it. He often basked in the memory of his past, relating anecdotes from his time there. I enjoyed listening to these stories. They gave me a sense of his likes, dislikes, hobbies and interests. He took a keen interest in my hobbies, interests and things I loved to do too. He never looked away when we talked.

Over the next few weeks, I became quite close to him and his family. We definitely shared something. Something more than just friendship. I did not tell him how I felt because I expected him to make the first move. My friend Soniya told me I was in love with him. Maybe I really was, but I wasn't sure. At times, I felt he didn't want to rush into anything. I wanted the same, but the desire to be close to him became more intense as the days passed.

I craved to be in his company or lock eyes with him in office. At home, I stalked him on Facebook for hours. At the dinner table, I only spoke about him and our time together. My parents soon realized I was crazily in love with him. One day, my father asked me if I wanted to marry him, and I instantly said yes. I just wanted to be with him and spend every moment of my life with him. I'd known him for almost a year now, and I couldn't be surer about my decision.

Finally, the day came when he asked me out on a date. It took me an entire day to decide what I would wear. I settled for a pink satin maxi dress and coiled my hair into a neat bun at the nape of my neck. My parents said I looked beautiful.

He picked me up from my place at 7 p.m. and then drove us to his favourite eatery in London, The Ledbury. Everything about him was extraordinary. Like a fine gentleman, he opened the door for me and led me inside the restaurant. Dressed in a camel-coloured blazer and beige pants, he looked breathtakingly handsome. I couldn't take my eyes off him.

'I'm sorry I didn't ask if you wanted to come here or not,' he said as he pulled out a chair for me.

'It's your favourite place. Why wouldn't I want to come here?' I replied, smiling at him.

My cheeks crimsoned when I realized he was looking at me. He always had this effect on me.

'What's the name of your favourite restaurant here?' he asked, resting his elbows on the table and leaning forward.

'Oh, there are so many. Original Lahore Restaurant, Hard Rock Café, The Barbary . . . etc. etc.'

'Next time, we'll go to a place of your choice,' he said as he picked up the menu.

'Sure,' I said.

After we were done with dinner, he ordered a bottle of wine and poured himself a glass. He offered it to me but I refused. This was not the time to get carried away. I wanted to know what else he had planned for us tonight. His eyes bored into mine as he sipped his drink. I returned his intent gaze, my cheeks turning a deep shade of crimson in the process. Suddenly, muffled giggles snapped me out of my trance, and I turned around to see what was happening. A group of girls, seated at the table behind us, were looking at Aariz and smiling flirtatiously. I felt a sharp pang of jealousy. He sensed my discomfort and turned around to see what was causing it. He looked at the girls and then back at me, and I did the same. Both of us stared at each other for a second and then burst out laughing.

'You know, sometimes, I hate it when women give me so much attention,' he said between laughs.

I continued to giggle.

'Don't they have anything else to talk about?'

'Well, they can't resist talking about you, maybe?'

'No, but I don't like it,' he said matter-of-factly.

'I always thought men enjoyed getting attention from women,' I said, clearing my throat.

'Yeah, they do, but I don't. It's high time mindsets change.'

'What do you mean?' I asked.

'I mean, isn't it quite stereotypical, girls going after guys and vice versa?'

'What?' I laughed at his question.

'What happened?' He shrugged.

'That's how it has always been. Men chasing women. Women chasing men. It's natural. A universal truth.'

'Okay, if you say so,' he said, rolling his eyes.

We left the restaurant and walked towards the car.

I shivered as the cold air hit me and regretted not bringing my shawl.

'Are you okay?' he asked, his brows furrowed in concern.

'I'm fine,' I lied.

'No, you're shivering.'

Before I could say another word, he took off his camel-coloured blazer and wrapped it around my shoulders. I inhaled his perfume as he leaned closer, sending shivers down my spine. I slightly turned my head to look at his face—his almond-brown eyes, the long lashes, his perfectly shaped nose and his sensual lips. He was perfect.

'Are you okay now?' he whispered, his breath intermingling with mine.

'Yes,' I whispered back, looking into his dreamy eyes.

'Good,' he said, looking back into mine.

Both of us made our way to the car. We remained quiet during the journey homewards, lost in our respective dreamworlds.

'We're here,' he declared as he brought the car to a halt outside my house. There was a pregnant pause as we both looked ahead at the road.

'Thank you for the lovely evening, Aariz. I had a great time,' I finally said, turning my face towards him.

'Thank you for coming,' he said, smiling.

'Umm, I should return your jacket. Wait,' I said, holding the front lapel.

'It's okay.' He held my hand. My heartbeat stopped. 'You can keep it. I'll take it some other time.'

'Sure?' I asked, my voice softer than a whisper.

'Of course, Zynah.' He smiled.

I wrapped my fingers around his hand and inched closer, closing the gap between us. Slowly, I put my arms around his neck and looked into his eyes.

'Zy . . .'

Before he could say my name, I pressed my lips against his and slowly devoured them. He shifted in his seat, wrapping his arms around the small of my back. I leaned closer, deepening our kiss. I could not make out whether he was kissing me back with the same intensity or not. The feeling was exhilarating yet beautiful. I could live in this moment for an eternity.

Suddenly, the silence was pierced by a loud screech of brakes, He jerked his head up, interrupting the kiss. I flushed as I realized what I'd just done. I stole a glance at him but he was busy looking at the car that had stopped with a loud thud. I searched his face for a reaction but he remained impassive.

'Uh, maybe I should just leave,' I said, picking up my handbag.

'All right,' he mumbled.

I got out of the car and slung the handbag over my shoulder.

'Zynah,' Aariz said.

I turned around to look back at him.

'Goodnight,' he said, smiling.

'Goodnight,' I said before hurrying inside my house.

I shut the door behind me and collapsed on the floor. *What did I just do? Did I really kiss Aariz Kamran? Oh God! Where did that courage come from? But . . . did he . . . did he kiss me back? Of course, he did. I think I'm going mad . . . Does love really make you this crazy?* I wondered.

🎧

The next morning, my parents quizzed me about the previous night. They wanted a blow-by-blow account of how the evening panned out. Honestly, I didn't know what to tell them. I was as confused as they were. Aariz had not proposed to me or professed his love but something had surely happened between us and that made me believe that he was interested.

'Did anything happen last night?' my mother asked, standing on the threshold of the kitchen. 'Did he say something to you?' she asked again when I didn't respond.

'Mummy, please!' I shot her a fuming look and stormed out of the kitchen.

'What's wrong with you? Tell me, did something happen?' she asked, following me to the dining table.

'What do you want to know?' I asked her as I spread peanut butter on a slice of toast.

'Did he say something?' she asked again.

'Um, no,' I said, shaking my head.

'Did he do something?' She raised a brow.

'Mummy!' I frowned.

'Then what happened?' she asked, getting impatient. 'Tell me, na.'

'I think, he likes me too,' I finally said.

'You think?' she asked. Right then, my father joined us at the dining table.

I nodded, biting into the toast.

'Do you want me to talk to Kamran?' Daddy asked, taking a seat beside me.

'Wait, what will you ask him?' I asked.

'I will ask him if his son is interested in marrying my daughter and see if we can fix a date.'

'Daddy, really?' I asked, blushing scarlet.

'I didn't know girls still blushed on hearing about their marriage,' Daddy teased me.

'Malik Sahib, stop wasting your time. Go and talk to Kamran bhai and see what he says. I'm sure Aariz must have spoken to his parents by now,' Mummy said.

'Okay, madam. I will,' Daddy said.

'I love you, Mummy!' I stood up and wrapped my arms around her.

'I can't wait to see you as a bride, my darling!'

The Never-Ending Wait

When Daddy spoke to Uncle Kamran the next day, he said that Aariz wanted to settle down eventually but right now marriage was not his priority. He had a lot on his mind what with his new life in London and the family business. He wanted to focus on these aspects for now and hadn't given marriage a thought. I felt dejected when I learnt of this. He had made me feel so special the other day. I was under the impression that he was in love with me and couldn't wait to get married. However, I was wrong. In fact, when I met him the next time, he acted nonchalant about the entire situation. He didn't even mention our date or the kiss or the fact that my father had asked his father about our marriage. He greeted me cordially and then went about his work. I was taken aback by his strange behaviour. Why was he acting like this, like nothing had happened between us? I was confused. And I wanted answers. I wanted to know why he had forged a close bond with me if he wasn't even interested. I wanted to know if he was involved with someone else. During the lunch break, I barged into his cabin, taking him by surprise.

'Zynah! Come in,' he said animatedly.

'I hope I am not disturbing you,' I said, taking a seat opposite him.

'You can never disturb me,' he said, leaning forward.

'Thanks,' I said, tucking my hair behind my ears.

'Want some coffee?'

'Sure,' I murmured.

He picked up his telephone and ordered two cups of coffee.

'So, how's work going? I hope Anna is training you well.'

Anna, the senior graphic designer, was my mentor.

'Yeah, she is,' I said with a weak smile. I had not come here to discuss my training. I wanted to talk about us. 'Uh, I . . .' I didn't know how to start.

'Is everything okay?' he asked, concerned.

'Actually, I came here to talk to you . . . about the other night,' I said at last.

He slowly shifted in his seat, his face composed.

'Aariz, I know Uncle Kamran and Daddy have had a conversation. I just wanted to know what you feel about it. About us . . . about our marr . . .'

'Listen, Zynah.' He cut me in between. I looked at him, my face solemn. 'It's not what you think, okay? I like you. In fact, I like you a lot. I feel good when you're around.'

I felt a bit relieved to know he liked me.

'But I don't want to settle down right now. Don't you think it's too early for both of us? Perhaps, we should get to know each other more.'

I looked at him again, confused.

'But we have spent so much time together. You still think you don't know me?' I asked him.

'Zynah . . .' He snorted. 'It's not only about me. How well do you know me?'

'I know everything about you!' I exclaimed.

'No, Zynah. You don't,' he said, shaking his head.

'What?' I asked, baffled.

'You think you know me but you don't. You've only known me for a year.'

'Isn't that enough?'

'It's never enough, Zynah. Trust me,' he said.

I felt helpless. I did not know what to say or how to convince him.

'So,' he said, clearing his throat. 'I'd like to give our relationship some time before we get married. We have to be sure that this is what we want. Because I don't want us to regret this for the rest of our lives,' he declared.

'Aariz, I won't regret marrying you. I am sure about that!' I insisted.

'I want you to think about it, Zynah. Please try to understand?' He put his hand on mine and I shivered slightly. 'Plus, I have other things on my mind right now. I have to take this company forward. Strive hard for it. So, please.'

I looked at him in despair. I could not say anything else to convince him, so I gave up. Heaving a sigh, I nodded at him.

'Thank you, Zynah,' he whispered, his eyes gleaming. 'Let's just wait for the right time. Okay?'

I nodded at him again, not sure how to respond.

I walked out of his cabin, feeling drained. Perhaps I was not someone he was looking for. Maybe I lacked something. Maybe I wasn't perfect. Then why had he said he wanted more time? Perhaps he did like me but did not want to get married right away. He never said he did not like me or was in love with someone else. Couldn't I give him what he wanted? Couldn't I give him more time? Of course I could. I could do anything for him. Anything.

I told my parents not to panic about the situation and just wait for the right time as Aariz had said. I knew we would get married eventually. Till that time, I would wait—for him to make up his mind, for him to understand me better, for him to say yes.

For Old Friendship's Sake

I wondered what kind of a person I had become since Aariz had come into my life. I had never behaved like this before—clingy or desperate for a man's attention. I did not like the person I was turning into but it wasn't in my control. I decided to keep myself busy and focus more on my job and social life. We met every other day in office but we never spoke about our issues. Instead, we discussed work. He did ask me out a couple of times, but I politely refused. From his expression, it was clear he knew I was upset. He could sense a change in my attitude towards him. Still he never asked me the reason or made any effort to change things. I spent my weekends with my friends—hanging out at local pubs, catching movies in theatres, going out for shopping, or trying out new eateries. And, of course, whenever I wanted some me time, I went to my favourite music store or sat in the church for hours.

But things changed one night. I was at a local pub for my friend's birthday party when I bumped into an old school friend from Lahore—my captain, Rehaan, the one who used to give me driving classes. I can't explain

140

how happy I felt when I saw him that night. I caught him taking my pictures, and the moment he laid eyes on me, he blushed. He hadn't changed much. Despite a well-built body and a light stubble, he looked almost the same. He had grown taller over the years and turned into a handsome man. But he pretended not to recognize me and walked away. Then I noticed that a few of my friends were bullying him and intervened. Before he could apologize, I left the party.

Thank God, he turned up the next day at the music store and apologized to me. I was glad he enjoyed my company as much as I did his. If it wasn't for him, I wouldn't have been able to come out of my shell. I laughed, danced, drank and acted wild when I was with him. There was no awkwardness between us.

I didn't know I could open up to someone, especially a guy, so easily but Rehaan made that possible. When I had a terrible day at work, I called up Rehaan to make plans. He filled the void that Aariz had left in my life. He made me happy, he made me laugh. But most importantly, he made me forget the pain Aariz had given me. It took me some time to realize that I was again becoming the person I used to be. With Rehaan, I felt like my old self.

I had somewhat made peace with what life had offered me. Instead of whining about it, I had stopped caring about the world and lived every day, every moment like it was my last. Until one night, when Daddy broke the news that Aariz had agreed to marry me. He had given his consent to his parents.

My World Turned Topsy-Turvy

I had gone out partying with Rehaan. One tequila shot turned into several and by the time I tiptoed into my living room, the first rays of the sun were streaming in. The silhouettes of my parents sitting at the dining table startled me.

'Um, hi, guys. You're up early,' I said as I kept my bag in a corner and switched on the lights. *Thank God, I am not too drunk*, I thought.

'Zynah, where were you?' Daddy asked, his face contorted with concern.

'Sorry, I was at the club with my friend Rehaan,' I told them, taking off my leather jacket.

'We have some news for you, Zynah,' Mummy cut in.

'What?' I asked, looking at their faces.

'Kamran called. Aariz has agreed to marry you.'

The jacket fell from my hand and landed on the floor with a light thud. My heartbeat quickened and tears welled up in my eyes as I slowly took in what I'd just heard.

'We're so happy for you, honey,' Mummy said and wrapped her arms around me. I stood like a statue, still surprised.

'You're happy, right?' Daddy asked, observing my reaction.

I freed myself from Mummy's embrace and wiped the tears off my face.

'Yes, I am.' I nodded at him, trying to smile.

A little later, I plonked myself on my bed, wondering how Aariz had agreed to marry me. It had almost been a year since we had had that discussion in his office. I had thought he would take longer to decide. But perhaps knowing a girl for two long years was enough for him. I felt a sudden urge to talk to him, to hear his voice. I took a deep breath before dialling his number. I wanted him to tell me that he loved me; that he was ready to marry me.

'Zynah?' he whispered huskily.

A shiver ran down my spine when I heard his throaty voice.

'Aariz . . .' I whispered. I still didn't understand why his voice made me go weak in the knees. Fresh tears sprang from my eyes and I sniffed.

'Zynah, what's wrong? Are you okay?' he asked, his voice filled with concern.

'Did you . . . did you say yes?' I managed to ask.

There was a long pause before he replied. 'Yes, I did,' he answered.

I closed my eyes, taking in his reply. Tears streamed down my cheeks, but I did not wipe them off.

'Zynah, are you there?' he asked when he didn't get a response. 'Zynah?'

'Yes, I'm here,' I whispered.

'I tried calling your number but it was switched off. Where were you all night?'

'I'm sorry. I was out with a friend.'

'Okay . . . let's talk about this in office. All right?'

'Yeah, okay,' I said, wiping my face with the back of my hand.

'See you then. Goodnight.'

'Goodnight,' I said and ended the call.

I wondered if I should call Rehaan and tell him what had just happened. I felt bad for hiding the truth from him for so long. I should have told him about Aariz when we first met. I knew he was upset because I hadn't been honest with him. He was my friend and had every right to know what was happening in my life. Apart from that, I felt miserable about making him drink too much. Would he remember anything I told him about Aariz when he woke up?

I closed my eyes in an attempt to quieten my mind. I hadn't expected Aariz to agree so soon. I wondered what had made him change his mind. What had made him say yes.

Later in the day, I dialled Rehaan's number to check on him. The tone of his voice told me that he was upset. I tried to apologize and even accepted my mistake but he wasn't ready to listen. Before I could tell him about the recent developments, he made an excuse and hung up.

I met Aariz in office the same day. He looked fresh and *happy*. I could not figure out if he was genuinely happy or had plastered a fake smile on his face. My colleagues had gathered around my seat and the minute I arrived, they started throwing confetti on me and breaking party poppers. I was taken aback. Why did Aariz tell the others? Why was he embarrassing me? It was all so awkward. My colleagues congratulated me one by one. It was hard for me to tell how many were genuinely happy and how many were jealous. Aariz and

Uncle Kamran stood a few feet away, looking at me and smiling. I tucked my hair behind my ears and smiled back.

🎧

'Why did you agree?' I asked Aariz as he drove us to a nearby restaurant for lunch.

'What do you mean?' he asked.

I studied his perfect profile for a few seconds before answering, 'I thought you wanted . . . time to be sure about us . . .' I said finally.

'Aren't two years enough?' he asked, giving me a sidelong glance.

'Are you sure about us now? About me?' I asked, pressing my lips together.

'I was always sure about you, Zynah.' He turned to look at me and smiled.

'Then why didn't you agree earlier?'

'Perhaps, I wasn't ready . . . for a commitment; ready for marriage; ready to share my life with someone.'

'And now you are?' I raised my brows.

'I guess I am,' he said as he pulled the car into the parking lot before bringing it to a complete stop.

He turned to look at me, taking my hand in his. 'Zynah, I really love my family . . . and those who are dear to me. Including you,' he said.

'My parents think I'd be happy with you and your parents think the same. Moreover, both of us like each other and believe we can become good life partners. I've always listened to my parents. I've never said no to them. When they asked me to get married to you, I didn't say no. I just asked for more time. And, now I think I'm ready for this responsibility. I'm ready to start a new relationship. With you.'

My lips curved into a smile but it did not reach my eyes. There was something amiss; it was not how I had imagined it.

'Miss Zynah Malik, will you marry me?' he asked, leaning closer.

I grinned at his gesture and instantly nodded.

'Thank you.' He pulled my hand to his lips and gently kissed it.

🎧

My parents were more thrilled about the news than I was. I was happy; I was over the moon but just couldn't bring that to my face. Something felt off. I couldn't put a finger on it. When I discussed my mixed emotions with my friend Soniya, she thought I'd gone mad. She said perhaps I was getting cold feet. I wanted to believe her; I wanted to believe that it was a bout of anxiety and nothing else. I tried to convince myself—this is what I had wanted. I was happy; happy to spend the rest of my life with Aariz. The man of my dreams.

I tried to contact Rehaan over the next couple of days but he seemed busy with his exams. Or, maybe, he was ignoring me. One night, I decided to pay him a surprise visit. I drove up to his apartment and texted him to come downstairs. But when he did, I started laughing. He looked funny in his pyjamas. Funny and cute. I almost felt like getting out of the car and giving him a bear hug. When I asked him why he was not answering my calls, he gave the same old excuse—he was busy with exams. But his behaviour did not seem normal. In the past, no matter how busy he was, he had always taken out time for me. I tried to talk to him but he remained cold and unresponsive, so I just left. The next day, he apologized for his stupidity, and since I couldn't stay mad at him for long, I relented. We made up over cones of ice cream. Everything was fine until he brought up Aariz again. He asked me if I was sure about him; if I really loved him. When I said I did, he went off on a different tangent and started asking if Aariz felt the same way or not. I wanted to tell Rehaan that Aariz and I were in a relationship, that we were getting married. But he did not give me a chance to speak and continued to rebuke me. I didn't expect this from him. He was my friend. At least he should have understood my feelings. But he hurt me; hurt my sentiments. I told him not to interfere with my life and stormed off.

One night, just as I was getting ready for bed, I got a call from a guy named Vikram. He introduced himself as Rehaan's flatmate and said he had something important to tell me—it was about Rehaan. He had had too much to drink and had almost got himself killed. Vikram had saved him in the nick of time and brought him home. He was in bad shape and was mumbling my name in his sleep. Vikram wanted me to come down to their apartment. He said he was worried that Rehaan was not in his right mind. I drove at breakneck speed and reached their apartment in no time. I did not go inside and waited for Rehaan on the front porch. As soon as he came out, I started bombarding him with questions, rebuking him for behaving recklessly. But I was shocked into silence by his reply. He said he was in love with me; that he had been in love with me since we were in school. I was appalled by this sudden revelation and tried to reason

with him. But he retaliated and tried to forcibly kiss me.
When I pushed him away, he started hurling abuses at
Aariz. I couldn't take it any more. I just got into my car
and drove off, leaving him to his own devices.

Later that night, I curled up in bed and cried for
hours. I'd lost a friend whom I considered an integral
part of my life, whom I trusted with my life.

The Wedding

On the brighter side, our wedding date had been fixed. I couldn't wait to start a new life with Aariz. Our wedding happened in a jiffy. I had expected a grand affair because Uncle Kamran had a lot of friends in London. But, he chose to keep it small by inviting only his close friends and family. We had invited our immediate relatives from Lahore. My elder brother, Zayn, was specially flying down from Australia to be a part of the celebration, but his wife had refused to accompany him. This made Mummy very unhappy.

Two days before the main day, we held a small mehndi ceremony at our house where I invited all my close friends. I missed Rehaan, but I knew I couldn't call him. I hadn't even told him I was getting married. Maybe this was the right thing to do. Maybe there was no place for him in my life.

The nikah was to take place in a local mosque followed by a grand reception. Finally, the day was upon us. Aariz, along with his close male friends and relatives, sat across from me, a see-through curtain separating us. I stole a coy glance at him. He was a vision in an off-white sherwani. I couldn't believe I was marrying this gorgeous man. I had waited for this moment for so long and it was finally happening. Maulvi Sahib asked Aariz for his consent. He looked in my direction, grinned and then said, 'Qubuul hai.' I tingled with excitement on hearing those magical words. But I was also nervous. The question, *Had I made the right decision*, was still troubling me deep down. I knew there was no turning back from here. I tried to quieten my mind but the thoughts persisted. I felt sick to my stomach but tried to suppress the feeling.

Maulvi Sahib turned to me and asked the same question. But my head whirred with irrational fear and I couldn't bring myself to answer. Mummy, who was sitting beside me, mouthed the words with a gesture of her hand. I looked at her gleaming face and then back at Aariz, who still had a wide grin on his face. I took a deep breath and finally whispered, 'Qubuul hai.' A tear escaped my eye as Mummy embraced me in a warm hug.

Since the reception was on the same day, we hurried back to Aariz's house, my house, in Mallord Street, after the nikah. Aariz followed me into our room, which was decorated with colourful flowers and fairy lights, and then locked the door from inside. My heart thumped loudly in my chest as I took in the decor.

'Why don't you sit on the bed and relax for a bit? I'll go and change,' he said.

I waited for him with bated breath, my body burning with desire.

After a few minutes, he came into the room looking fresh. He combed his fingers through his hair as he sat beside me, his eyes not leaving mine.

'Do you want to change?' he asked.

'Uh, yeah. I have to get ready for the reception,' I managed to say, my lips quivering with nervousness.

'Want me to help you get rid of the jewellery and . . . clothes?' he asked, getting up. I stood up too, his words making me a little dizzy.

'No, I, uh . . . I'll manage,' I said.

'Come, let's take this dupatta off your head.' I gave him a sidelong glance as he removed the countless bobby pins from my hair and fell in love all over again. His eyes soon met mine, making me go weak in the knees. He took the dupatta off and held my face in his hands. I closed my eyes and waited for his warm lips to touch mine. But before he could kiss me, a loud knock on the door interrupted the moment. It was Aariz's mother.

'Hey, Mom!' he said, planting a kiss on her forehead.

'I hope I've not disturbed you,' she said, winking at us.

'Of course not, Aunty,' I mumbled, lowering my head.

'Please call me Mom. No more Aunty. Okay?'

I nodded in agreement.

'Here you go. This is the dress you'll be wearing tonight at the party. The jewellery is also inside the packet,' she said, handing me a decorated basket.

'This looks beautiful. Thank you,' I said gratefully.

'The guests will start arriving by 7 p.m. Make sure you both get ready by then.'

'Sure, Mom,' Aariz said, leaning against the door.

'Zynah, I've hired a make-up artiste for you. She'll be here in ten minutes,' she said as she exited the room.

Later in the evening, I sat in front of the mirror, taking off my jewellery in a slow and thoughtful manner. The reception party had been a grand affair—Uncle Kamran had invited all his colleagues, friends and relatives. Aariz looked striking in a black suit, which he had paired with a blue shirt and tie.

After standing on the stage all evening, meeting all and sundry, I felt exhausted and yearned to hit the bed. Thankfully, the party was soon over and after bidding goodbye to my parents and brother, I came home with Aariz and his parents.

I was halfway up the staircase when I realized Aariz was not following me. I craned forward to see where he was and saw him sitting with his parents in the living room. He looked up and said, 'You please go up. I have some work to finish. I will see you in a bit.'

It had been an hour since but he had still not come up.

Suddenly my phone beeped, piercing the silence. I looked around and saw it was lying on the bed. Amongst millions of messages and missed calls, Aariz's message caught my eye. Why was he texting me?

There's a black lacy nightie in the walk-in cupboard. Please wear that tonight.

My cheeks crimsoned as I read the message. I read it again and again until my head reeled. I found the black lacy nightie, carefully wrapped in a baby-blue paper, on one of the shelves of the walk-in cupboard. The sight of the garment brought a coy smile to my face. I imagined Aariz's expression when he saw me in it. The thought aroused me. I slowly took off my clothes and stepped into the shower. I slathered on some moisturizer before slipping into the nightie. I examined myself in the mirror. I had never worn a lacy nightdress before and felt a bit self-conscious. But why was I scared? Isn't this what I wanted? Putting my fears aside, I picked a fine-toothed comb and ran it through my silky, straight hair. I put on some make-up and sprayed some perfume on. Gathering my courage, I unlocked the door and stepped into the room. To my astonishment, the room was bathed in darkness. Only a small lamp glowed in a corner. I could make out Aariz's silhouette on the bed and hear his gentle snores. A lump formed in my throat and I lowered my eyes to hide my disappointment. I had never felt so humiliated in my life. Before he could wake up and see me in the nightie, I rushed inside the washroom and closed the door behind me. How could he just fall sleep without telling me? When did he come into the room? He knew I was going to wear the nightie. Couldn't he have waited for me a bit longer? He had ruined our first night together.

The Honeymoon

I woke up to an empty bed the next morning. The curtains had been drawn back, allowing a shaft of sunlight into the room. I sat up and rested my head against the headboard. I scanned th room but Aariz was nowhere to be seen. There was no movement in the washroom which meant he was probably downstairs. A small note and a bunch of fresh red roses were kept on the side table. I slowly picked up the note and unfolded it.

> Good morning, Wife
> I'm sorry about last night. I don't know when I fell asleep. I promise I will make it up to you. There's an ivory dress inside your closet. Be ready by 1 p.m. I'll pick you up and we'll go out for lunch. Till then, enjoy the red roses.
> Love,
> Your Husband

A smile lit up my face and the rush of anger I had felt the previous night disappeared. I made my way to the walk-in cupboard to look for the dress. It was as beautiful as

I had imagined it to be. I quickly got dressed and made my way downstairs to find Uncle Kamran and Aunty Raima at the dining table. I told them about the lunch plan but they already knew about it. Aariz was known to be punctual, and he was there on time. He wanted to take me to one of my favourite restaurants.

'Let's go to a place neither of us has tried before,' I suggested as he drove the car.

'Fair enough.'

'I've been dying to try Seven Park Place. Have you been there?'

'No. I don't think so. Shall we go there?'

'Yes. Why don't you look it up on Google Maps?'

'Sure. Let me check.'

After lunch, we drove around aimlessly, talking and listening to music. I was ecstatic when he surprised me with news about our honeymoon. He was taking me to Italy—a place that had been on his wish list for a long time. I did feel a twinge of disappointment as I had thought it would be somewhere more exotic like Switzerland, Paris or Cape Town. But I didn't want to be a killjoy, since he had already applied for our visas and bought the tickets. We were scheduled to leave the following day so he asked me to pack as soon as we returned home. I was thrilled. Overjoyed. Why wouldn't I be? I was living the life I'd always wanted.

I met my parents before leaving and could see how happy they were for me and the life I was leading. It all seemed perfect. Or at least that's what we all thought at that point.

Aariz had outdone himself by booking a lavish honeymoon suite in one of the finest hotels in Florence. I was stunned by the opulence of the rooms, the contemporary furniture and the soothing colour palette of white and greys. The balcony, which overlooked Ponte Vecchio, was adorned with colourful hanging baskets and planters. I stood there for a few seconds, drinking in the view, and then came back and plonked myself on the bed.

'Tired already?' Aariz asked, as he placed his suitcase on the luggage rack.

'Yeah, a little bit,' I said.

'You should get some sleep.'

'I think . . . *We* should get some sleep,' I said as I played with a stray strand of hair coquettishly. It was our honeymoon after all.

'Well.' He smiled in return and stepped closer. My heartbeat quickened. 'I know you're tired, love.' He caressed my cheek with his warm hand. 'I want you to rest before we go out and see this beautiful city. Meanwhile, I'll go out and finish a business meeting and when I come back I want you to be ready in your prettiest dress.' He withdrew his hand from my face and turned around.

'Business meeting?' I sat up. 'What are you talking about? You're going for a meeting? Here?' I was stunned.

'Yes. I planned it that way,' he said, putting his cell phone in his pocket.

'But . . . but . . . we are here on our honeymoon, not a business trip.' I frowned.

'I know, love. It's only going to take an hour and then I'll be back.'

'Did you select this place because of your meeting?' I asked him, my face solemn.

'What? No!' He laughed. 'Of course not. The meeting was impromptu. I have to meet designers from a very prestigious interior design company. If all works out,

one of them might become a partner. Anyway, I have to
go now. You get some sleep and then get ready before I
come back. See you.' Before I could say anything, he left
the room.

I felt disappointed. To distract myself, I opened
Snapchat and posted a story about the beautiful view.
Then I called Mummy and told her that we had reached
safely and I was already missing them. I tried to sleep
but couldn't close my eyes for more than a few minutes.
I was suddenly scared of being alone in the room. It was
uncomfortably silent. I looked at my watch every few
minutes or strained my ears for approaching footsteps.
It had already been two hours and Aariz had still
not returned. I decided to wait a little longer before
giving him a call. I opened one of our suitcases and
picked out a cool summer dress for the evening. Then
I undressed and stepped into the shower. I stood under
it and let the water run down my back. It calmed me
down a little. I thought I heard the click of the door and
quickly wrapped myself in a towel before running out.
But Aariz was still not back. I took out my cell phone
and dialled his number. After a few rings, his number
became unreachable. I tried his number again and again
but couldn't get through. Tears welled up in my eyes. I
wiped them off and typed a message. Maybe he would
see that and call me back. He had been away for three
long hours. If he was going to be late, he should have
informed me. I looked at myself in the mirror and
realized that the mascara was smeared all over my face.
I sat down, wallowing in self-pity. I didn't know how
to contact him. All I knew was that he had gone to
attend a business meeting but I did not know where.
After another hour passed, I decided to go downstairs

and inquire about him at the help desk. Perhaps they knew his whereabouts. Maybe he hadn't even left the hotel. Maybe they had booked one of the conference halls here. With these thoughts, I rushed out of the room. I reached the help desk and asked if they knew where my husband had gone for his meeting. I showed them his picture on my phone and reminded them that we'd checked in a few hours ago. They remembered his face but had not seen him leave the hotel, which meant that he was still here. I felt a bit relieved. I decided to look for him and went around the hotel, checking every lounge, bar, club, restaurant, shop. I also peeped into the conference room. What if the client was staying in this very hotel and they were having the meeting in his room? I couldn't go around checking each room, so I gave up.

I contemplated calling either Aunty Raima or Uncle Kamran but that would just aggravate the situation. What was so important that he had completely forgotten about me? He knew I was alone in the room. Was he still at the meeting or had something happened to him? Concern and worry gripped me and I felt drained of energy. I slumped into the bed and curled up, hugging my knees. I don't remember for how long I lay in that position. I woke up when I heard the click of the door. I sat up and looked around. Aariz, still looking fresh, walked into the room and smiled at me. I quickly got off the bed and ran towards him.

'Hey . . . I'm sorry, I'm late . . .' he said, but before he could utter another word, I started pummelling him with my fists, my face contorted with fury.

'Zynah, what are you doing?' he asked, laughing at my childish behaviour.

Hearing him laugh made me angrier and I punched him harder.

'Okay, Zynah, stop now. It's hurting me! I said I'm sorry!'

'Why weren't you answering my calls? Why, why why?' I screamed.

When I didn't stop, he caught hold of my arms.

'Ouch!' I squealed in pain.

'Okay, enough now, Zynah,' he said in an irritated voice. 'I have already apologized. I was having a meeting in the basement of a building and there was no network there,' he said, tightening his grip around my arms and digging his fingernails into my skin.

'Aariz . . .' I whimpered as fresh tears rolled down my cheeks.

'What?' he asked.

'You're hurting me.'

He immediately released me and his expression softened.

'I'm sorry, love,' he whispered, holding my face in his hands. 'I'm really sorry. I promise I won't do this again.'

'It's . . . okay.' I shook my head.

I did not understand what he meant by that. He wouldn't leave me alone or hurt me again? I was confused, my head hurt. He pulled me closer and wrapped his arms around me. I did not hug him back because I was still in a state of shock. Everything seemed like a lie.

'Let's freshen up and go get dinner. My stomach is rumbling with hunger,' he said casually and walked towards the bathroom, leaving me there.

I was still shaking and tried to calm myself down. I looked at the marks his nails had left on my bare arms and then slowly walked up to the mirror to get a better look. The person who stared back was certainly not me. She was someone else. She was a mess.

♫

He took me to a local restaurant nearby for dinner. He was starving but I had lost my appetite. I was still angry at him. I knew confronting him wouldn't change anything as he'd already given an explanation and also apologized. But was it enough? No, it wasn't. I didn't want an apology; I wanted attention, care, love.

He didn't utter a word throughout. I looked at him in silence as he stuffed his face with food.

'Why aren't you eating?' he asked between mouthfuls, his voice indifferent.

'I guess I'm not hungry,' I said, looking away.

'I thought you were starving. C'mon, eat something.'

'I said I'm not hungry,' I shot back.

He stopped eating and looked up. 'Zynah, I know I've done something that I shouldn't have and I have already apologized. For how long are you going to punish me like this?'

'What did you say? Punish?' I said with a smirk. 'Am I punishing you?'

'Yeah,' he said, putting away his napkin. The irritation was back in his voice.

I looked away, my eyes welling with tears.

'I'm sorry, Zynah. I really am,' he said and put his hand on mine. 'I swear I will never do it again. Please don't ruin this trip. Please.'

I sniffed, withdrawing my hand.

'Thank you. Will you please finish your dinner now? Or should I do it on your behalf?' he said, flashing me a smile.

I smiled. 'Let's finish it together.'

The Night

We had been married for three days now but Aariz had not even touched me. In fact, we had not even kissed properly, let alone have sex. After dinner, we strolled back to the hotel, hand in hand. Before he could say anything, I slowly crawled into bed and closed my eyes.

'Tired already?' he asked as he sat beside me and ran his hand through my hair.

'Hmm,' I mumbled, my eyes closed. I liked what he did with my hair.

'Have a good night, love. Sleep well.' He kissed me and turned off the lamp.

I felt a pang of disappointment. I wanted him to lie next to me, to hold me in his arms. However, this time, I did not make the first move. I waited for him to initiate it. He could have easily told me not to sleep. Or he could have crawled into bed and taken me in his arms. But he did not do anything. He just sat on the couch with his laptop on his lap. I closed my eyes, feeling dejected once again.

It had been a week in Florence but things hadn't changed. Aariz had become more caring though, giving me his full time and attention. He did attend a few meetings in between and went out for two or three hours but kept me informed.

He took me to places only locals knew about, made sure I tried all the local cuisines and made me shop till I dropped dead. Despite all these efforts, I was unhappy. Something was amiss. We were in a platonic relationship. There was no intimacy between us. He still had not touched me the way I wanted him to.

One night, I decided to take matters in my own hands and make the first move. The table lamp cast long shadows on the walls. As usual, Aariz was sitting on the couch, his eyes fixed on his laptop. I changed into a deep red nightie. It not only accentuated my lean body but also made me look bold and beautiful. Perhaps a bit sexy too. Tucking my hair behind my ears, I stepped out of the washroom and looked at Aariz. He had still not noticed me. I slowly took a few steps in his direction, managing to distract him. His jaw fell open as he gawked at me from head to toe. Locking my eyes with him, I leaned forward and closed the lid of his laptop. He did not blink his eyes even once and neither did I. I put away the laptop on the coffee table and then slowly made my way towards him. I crawled on to the couch, spread my legs and sat on top of him, putting my arms around his neck. He smelled heavenly and it was enough to turn me on. I wondered if he was also equally turned on. I felt the sexual tension between us but his facial expression told me otherwise. He seemed a bit taken aback, slightly nervous. Perhaps he wasn't expecting me to make the first move, that too a bold one.

'I've been waiting for this moment for so long . . .' I whispered as I held him tightly, his face only a few inches away.

'Zynah . . .' he whispered.

Before he could say anything else, I pressed my lips against his and kissed them slowly. When we were a few seconds into the kiss, he parted his lips and took mine inside his mouth, playing with them with his tongue. It was enough for me to know that he also wanted this to happen. I hungrily searched for his tongue and teased it with mine before sucking it. This aroused him even more and he grabbed me by my waist and brought my body closer to his. I let out a deep moan and then nibbled his earlobe. He pulled my legs and wrapped them around his torso. Then, without breaking our intense kiss, he got up from the couch and carried me to the bed. I whimpered as he left my lips and kissed my neck. But then his lips found mine again. I pulled him harder towards me. He got the hint and lowered his body on top of mine. My hands found the button of his trousers and clutched it. When he realized I was struggling to unbutton it, he got up and hurriedly undressed himself. I feasted my eyes on his broad shoulders, muscled chest and tapering waist. I followed suit and took off my nightie. I wasn't wearing any undergarments under it and lay stark naked on my back, my eyes burning with desire. I saw pure lust in his eyes. He grabbed my ankles and pulled me towards him. I wrapped my legs around his hip as he lowered his body on mine, his hands cupping my breasts. I could feel his arousal and ached for him to be inside me.

'Zynah . . .' he breathed my name, his lips near my ear.

'Yes . . .'

'Are you sure about this?'

His unusual question startled me. 'What do you mean?'

'I mean . . . are you sure that you want to do this with *me*?'

'God. . . Aariz . . . are you crazy? I've been dying to do this with you.'

'What if I disappointed you? What if I'm not good at it?'

'You can never disappoint me.' Why was he saying these things?

'Are you sure?'

'I've never been surer,' I told him, holding his face in my hands and looking into his eyes. 'I love you.'

He let out a nervous laugh. 'I love you too.'

He sat up and looked at me with lustful eyes. He then leaned forward and pulled out a packet of condoms from the drawer of the bedside table. He tried to put it on but failed as he didn't have an erection.

'Aariz, what are you doing?' I whispered, getting slightly restless. 'Haven't you done this before? Are you a virgin?'

He jerked his head up, looking at me in surprise.

'What happened?' I asked him, grabbing his arm.

'I don't think it's happening, Zynah. I can't do it.'

'What?' I was shocked. 'What do you mean you can't do it?'

'I mean nothing. It's just not working right now.'

'Listen.' I held his arm tightly. 'Do not get anxious. Okay? Let's try in a few minutes. I'm sure it happens with every couple when they have sex for the first time.'

'No, Zynah. Let's just leave it. We should go to sleep. We can . . . we can try some other time. Not tonight, please.'

'Aariz . . .'

'Please, Zynah. Don't force me. I just don't feel like doing it tonight. Perhaps I'm not prepared. Please understand.' He looked at me pleadingly and I wondered what really was going on with him.

'But . . .' my voice trailed off.

'Thanks,' he muttered and picked up his clothes from the floor. He quickly got dressed and handed me my nightie.

'Please, wear it.'

I looked at him, completely flabbergasted. It felt like he was literally the 'first man on earth who was running away from sex. How could he leave me hanging? Grabbing my clothes from his hands, I sullenly stomped off to the washroom. I knew our honeymoon had ended.

Back to Reality

We never brought up that night again. In fact, both of us, mostly him, pretended like it never happened. More than being shocked, I was hurt by his nonchalant attitude. How could a mature and sensible man like Aariz behave the way he had in the past week? It all seemed so odd.

We stayed in Florence for another three days. We continued to share the same bed, but did not have sex. Sometimes, he would caress my hair or my arms to help me fall asleep. When he was in a cheerful mood, he would even plant kisses on my forehead, claim that he loved me but then turn to the other side and doze off. On most nights, my thoughts kept me awake. Did he not find me physically attractive? Why wasn't I able to arouse him? Did he not want me sexually? What was I missing? Was he involved with someone else? Or did he have performance anxiety? Or some other serious health issue? I soon began to fall into an abyss of depression. There were times when I wanted to confront him again and ask him what the problem was but held myself back as it would ruin his mood. I was scared I would humiliate or debase him in the process. Also, I didn't want to seem desperate. Maybe he needed more time. We shared the same bed, the same life, still we were strangers. The growing distance between us had started to worry me.

🎧

Our holiday was over and we were flying back to London the next day. My in-laws had come to receive us at the airport. I kept up a happy demeanour throughout. I didn't want them to think that we had issues. Aariz, on the other side, was delighted to see his parents. On our way home, Aunty Raima did notice my silence. She kept asking me about the trip and whether we'd enjoyed ourselves. Before I could utter a word, Aariz cut in and regaled his parents with a colourful account of the trip—how it was the best trip ever and how we had the time of our lives. I looked at his face in the rear-view mirror of the car and was stunned to see how perfectly he had masked the truth from his family. I had not enjoyed our honeymoon at all. In return, I was now ridden with angst and self-doubt. He passed me a sweet, saccharine smile when our eyes locked in the mirror and then looked ahead. Perplexed, I slowly sank into the back seat, wondering what kind of a person he really was. He continued to babble about the trip until we reached home.

Without bothering to see if he was following me or not, I dashed out of the car and headed straight to our room. I needed some time alone to gather my bearings. I was finally back in my city, away from the loneliness I had experienced in the past week. After calming myself down, I called my parents, informing them of my arrival. Mummy sounded extremely cheerful on the phone and invited us, Aariz and me, for lunch the next day.

'Hey, have you settled in?' Aariz asked, as he entered the room a few minutes later.

'Yes,' I said. 'I was . . . uh . . . speaking to Mummy on the phone. She has invited us for lunch tomorrow.'

'Sounds great.' He flashed me a smile. 'I'll take a quick shower.'

'Sure,' I nodded.

'By the way, Mom was asking about you. Please make sure you give her all the happy details about our honeymoon,' he said, before leaving the room.

I was stunned. So he was conscious of the fact that he had ruined our honeymoon.

'What do you mean?' I asked, holding the bathroom door.

'Well,' he sighed. 'What I meant was, just tell her what a lovely time we had in Florence. The places we visited, the food we had, the stuff we purchased, you know.'

'Is that it?' I asked, flinching.

'Is that it what?' he asked with a shrug.

'Aariz . . .' I took in a deep breath to regain my composure. 'Did we really have a lovely time in Florence?'

'Of course, sweetheart. We had a wonderful time. What made you think otherwise?'

What kind of a double-faced game was he playing with me? I narrowed my eyes, feeling as dejected and hopeless as ever. How could a man be so heartless? Was he really oblivious to my feelings or was he just pretending not to care?

'Anyway, I'm going for a shower. Please do as I say.' He quickly gave me a soft peck on the cheek and shut the bathroom door on my face.

I just stood there as the truth dawned on me—the reality was far from the life I'd imagined for myself.

Feeling dejected, I slowly changed my clothes and then went downstairs to meet my in-laws. At least they were nice and treated me like their own daughter. Aunty Raima asked the maid to bring tea with some freshly baked chocolate cookies.

'So, did you have a good time in Florence? I hope Aariz did not trouble you,' she said as she stirred her tea with a teaspoon.

Troublesome was an inappropriate word for a person like him. He had not troubled me; he had disappointed me, humiliated me.

'Yes, I did,' I said without any enthusiasm in my voice.

'Great. I'm just so glad that Aariz has finally settled down with a nice girl like you. You have no idea how many girls we made him meet in the last few years. None of them could win his heart. I don't know how you managed to change his views about marriage.'

'But why didn't he want to get married? Was he involved with someone whom you didn't approve of?' I asked her. This was the only topic that piqued my interest.

'I don't think so, Zynah. I've never seen Aariz with a girl. I can't even remember the name of the last girl he dated. He doesn't discuss his personal life with me,' Aunty Raima said thoughtfully, sipping her tea.

I didn't find any comfort in these revelations. They made me even more restless.

'We are a close-knit family. Even when he was in Canada, he would talk to Kamran and me every day but he never mentioned any girl. I asked him a few times if he had someone in mind, if he liked someone. We would have happily agreed if he had told us.'

I nodded in response, my mind more confused than before. If there was no other person in his life, then why was he behaving this way?

'Anyway, forget about all this. I'm happy that he chose you. Both of you look perfect with each other. A perfect match made in heaven.' Aunty Raima caressed my cheek, smiling.

I flashed a fake smile in response.

Later that day, we all were sitting at the dining table, eating dinner. Aariz finished his meal quickly and excused himself. He said he had some urgent work and rushed back to the room. I sat with my in-laws for a while, making small talk. When I yawned twice in a span of five minutes, Aunty Raima asked me to go back to my room and rest.

'I'll send over milk for both of you,' she told me.

'Sure. Goodnight,' I kissed her on her cheek.

When I entered the room, I found Aariz speaking to someone on the phone. He glanced at me warily as I closed the door behind me.

'Yeah, sure. I'll think about it and let you know,' he told the person at the other end of the line.

Ignoring him, I headed to the washroom to change my clothes. I thought he had come to the room to finish some important work but he was busy chit-chatting. Maybe he hadn't realized it yet, but I was beginning to lose my confidence in him. Or maybe I was losing confidence in myself. Wasn't he happy with me? Had his parents forced him to marry me? Or had I pushed him into this relationship? Why did he marry me if he wasn't interested? I was sure it wasn't because I was so keen on him. These thoughts were driving me crazy. I felt I was on the verge of a mental breakdown. I could not think of any person I could share my feelings with. Should I talk to my parents? Mummy? No, I couldn't discuss this with her because she already had enough problems of her own. I did not want her to have another panic attack because of me. Talking to Daddy wouldn't solve anything either. This was my decision after all. I had insisted on marrying Aariz. The truth was, I did not regret my decision even now. I saw this as a small hitch, and I was sure things would go back to normal in no time. Maybe I could discuss it with one of my close friends? Soniya? But then I thought against it. For a fleeting moment, Rehaan came to mind. However, I knew I couldn't talk to him either. He had betrayed me as a friend. He had ruined our friendship. This would only make him gloat. After all, that's what he wanted. I remembered that night on his porch when he had hurled abuses at Aariz. Had he really cursed me? Had his wish come true? I cleared my mind and thought harder till I settled on a solution. Since these were my problems, I had to deal with them myself. Discussing them with other people would only make the situation worse. The only person whose help I could seek was Aariz. I was having problems with him, his odd behaviour. He had to give me an explanation.

Aariz was already asleep when I came out of the washroom. Disappointed, I drank the glass of milk my mother-in-law had sent and got under the covers.

Please tell me why you're doing this to me, Aariz. Please . . .

The Emotional Breakdown

As usual, I woke up to an empty bed. Aariz had already gone downstairs. I could hear him talking to someone on the phone. I quietly climbed down the stairs to overhear the conversation but he saw me and ended the call abruptly.

'Hey,' he said, walking in my direction. It seemed as though he was hiding something behind his fake smile and this made me suspicious.

'Whom were you talking to?' I asked, folding my arms.

'Oh, it was someone from the office.'

'Why would people from office call you on a Sunday?'

'He wanted to discuss our upcoming project,' he said, smoothing down his eyebrow nervously.

I observed him for a few seconds, trying to assess whether he was telling the truth.

'May I know his name?' I asked.

'What? Why do you want to know his name? You don't trust me?' he asked, getting defensive.

'What has trust to do with this? I'm only asking his name!' I exclaimed.

'James. His name is James. He's our technical assistant. Happy now?' he said, glaring at me.

'Okay,' I mumbled, chewing my bottom lip.

'God. You're such a woman.' He walked away, shaking his head.

I decided to ignore the comment and get my day started. I went back to the room to have a cup of tea and get dressed. When I came down for breakfast, Aariz told me that he was going to the office to discuss the upcoming project with James. Though it seemed odd that he was going to office on a Sunday, I kept quiet and simply nodded. Aariz never worked on Sundays. This was unheard of, even when I was an employee there. After some time, I went to the living room where my in-laws were watching TV. When they inquired about Aariz, I told them he had gone to office to discuss a project with James.

'James? James Paul? Our technical assistant?' Uncle Kamran asked, peering at me through his glasses.

'I think so, yes,' I said.

'But he's not in town. He has gone to Georgia to attend a family event.'

I paled visibly on hearing this. Was he sure he was talking about the same James? Or had Aariz lied to me?

'Are you sure about that, Dad? I mean, you could also be mistaken . . .'

'No, beta,' he cut in. 'Our HR manager discussed his leave with me last week and I approved it. I am sure about it.'

If James Paul was in Georgia, then who was Aariz speaking to on the phone? And most importantly, why did he lie?

'Kamran Sahib, are you saying my son lied to Zynah?' Aunty Raima jumped into the conversation, getting defensive.

'I'm not saying that . . .'

'Well, that's what you meant!' she snapped. 'Zynah!' She turned to me. 'Please do not listen to Kamran. He might be mistaking James with someone else. Or maybe you heard incorrectly. He might have taken some other name.'

'No, Mom. Aariz told me about James,' I said, my voice low.

'There might be two technical assistants with the same name then. Isn't that possible?' she threw a sidelong glance at my father-in-law.

'Er . . . I don't think so,' he said, shaking his head.

'Whatever. Zynah, do not pay heed to such matters. Ask Aariz once again when he comes back. Now stop thinking so much and rest. I'll ask the maid to heat some food for you.' She smiled at me.

'Sure, okay,' I mumbled.

I was not convinced by Aunty Raima's theory. Aariz was definitely hiding something from me. As far as I knew, he never attended office on weekends and that too to meet a person who wasn't even in town. Something was not right. Was he having an affair? If yes, why did he tell me he loved me? Why the hell did he even marry me?

I paced the room, impatiently waiting for him to return. All sorts of thoughts rushed through my mind. I contemplated sending him a text message or giving him a call to clarify the matter but I hesitated every time I picked up the phone. It would be better to have a face-to-face conversation. Deep down, I sincerely prayed that he had not lied to me and had actually gone to the office to discuss a project with the said technical assistant. What would I do if I unearthed an ugly truth about him? I couldn't bring myself to believe that he had deceived me. As the minutes ticked by, I closed my eyes and curled up under the blanket. My subconscious mind was still alert, waiting for him to return.

My eyes flew open when I heard the click of the door. I sat up on the bed as Aariz quietly made his way into our room.

'You're still up?' he asked, keeping his wallet and wristwatch on the side table. 'I'm sorry I woke you up.' His eyes travelled to the glass of milk kept on the table.

'You haven't even had your milk. C'mon, finish it.'

I ignored his statement and looked straight at him.

'I think you're annoyed because I woke you up. Next time, I will be more careful.' He grinned at his own statement.

Unaffected by his flimsy line, I continued looking at him with a solemn expression which he conveniently ignored.

'I'll go and change.'

'Aariz, wait.' I got up from the bed and walked up to him.

'Yes?' He turned around to face me, his demeanour nonchalant.

'Where were you all day?'

'I told you I had to finish up some work at the office.'

'With James?' I raised a brow.

'Yes,' he said with a nod.

'But Dad told me James is vacationing in Georgia. So whom did you meet then?'

His face paled and he shifted his eyes nervously.

'What?' He frowned. 'No, uh . . . . Dad must have mistaken him with someone else.'

'It didn't seem like that. He was quite sure.'

'What are you implying?'

'Who were you with tonight, Aariz? Just tell me the truth.'

'You're calling me a liar?' He grimaced.

'I think I am,' I said, my face expressionless.

'C'mon, Zynah. You can't be that stupid.' He looked away, running a hand though his hair.

'Whom are you dating?' I asked him bluntly, my heart throbbing.

'Zynah, stop it, will you?' He tried to walk away from me but I held his arm.

'What are you doing? Have you gone crazy?' he frowned.

'Why don't you just tell me whom you were with?' I screamed as tears streamed down my cheeks.

'I told you, I was at work!' He raised his voice too.

'This explanation is not enough to justify what you're doing to me!' I said.

'What do you mean? What have I done to you?' he scowled.

'Why did you marry me if you didn't love me or weren't happy with me? Why?' I asked, grabbing his collar.

'God . . .' He shook his head as if he were disappointed in me.

'Answer me, Aariz! Do you think you can fool me with these lies? I am not blind or insane. I can sense everything that is happening around me. The way you treated me during our honeymoon was enough to open my eyes to reality. Time and again, your attitude has proved that you're not in love with me. You're interested in someone else.'

'Zynah . . . It's not what you think . . . Just listen to me,' Aariz tried to reason with me.

'What should I listen to? Another lie?' I said, stepping back. He heaved a sigh before he spoke again.

'Look Zynah, if you want to talk about it, then fine. Let's do this.'

For a moment, I became quiet. My body stilled. I did not know what was coming up. I did not even know if I was ready to listen to the truth yet.

'I know you're worried about our sex life, so let me come clean.'

I braced myself to hear him out.

'What I did to you during our honeymoon was unfair. I should not have offended you. However, at that time, none of that was in my control. I didn't mean to hurt your sentiments. It just happened like that. Perhaps there is a right time and a right place for everything.' He shrugged. 'It's as simple as that.'

His explanation did nothing to calm me down.

'Right time? Right place?' His words choked me.

He nodded.

'What are you talking about? Everything was damn right in that moment!' I said, regaining my composure.

'Lower down your voice, Zynah, please,' he said with a gesture of his hand.

'Stop telling me what to do!' I screamed.

He continued to stare at me for a few seconds and then shook his head.

'It was our honeymoon, dammit!' More tears rushed down from my eyes. 'But you chose to ruin everything for me, for us.'

'Zynah, why are you crying over this?' He inched closer and wrapped his arm around my shoulders. 'Please, don't cry.' He wiped off my tears.

'Is there someone else in your life?' I said, squirming in his embrace.

'Zynah, listen to me.' He tried to hold me again.

'Is there some other woman? Please tell me!' I broke into a loud sob.

'There is no other woman, Zynah. Trust me. There's no other woman. You're the only woman I've ever loved,' he declared, caressing my cheeks.

'Then why are you so distant from me? Why?'

'Trust me, I don't want to. This is not what I had planned either. Oh God. None of this is going right.' He stepped away from me, putting a hand over his forehead.

'Aariz, please don't go away from me. I can't bear this distance between us. I want you to be closer to me. I want us to feel complete. Please . . . don't go away. I love you.' I threw myself into his arms. 'I love you very much.' I continued to sob as I embraced him.

He held me back and looked into my eyes.

'Zynah . . .' He tucked a strand of hair behind my ear. 'I love you too.' It felt like he was trying to convince himself rather than me. 'Stop crying now, please.'

Before he could make another excuse or do anything else, I brought my face closer to his and kissed him. To my surprise, he kissed me back—not with the same urgency or intensity but he did. And in that moment, that's what mattered. He pulled back and looked into my eyes, our breaths uneven. He then held my hand and led me to our bed. I followed him like a lovesick puppy. He made me sit down and caressed my cheeks once again, his eyes filled with affection.

'Let me change. I'll be back in a minute.'

I held his hand tightly.

'Aariz, please. Not tonight.'

'I promise we'll make love tonight,' he said, his eyes sparkling.

I wanted to trust him. I wanted to believe his words.

'Meanwhile, you finish your milk. Be right back.' He quickly kissed me on my forehead and walked towards the bathroom.

I heaved a sigh of relief, tucking away my hair behind my ears. Perhaps I was overreacting. The way he convinced me that he loved only me and there was no other woman in his life was enough to overpower the doubts and uncertainly that had plagued my mind. For the first time since we got married, I felt content. I felt closer to what I wanted to conquer. I loved him and I wanted to feel this emotion physically. As I waited for Aariz to come back from the bathroom, I took the glass of milk kept on my bedside table and quickly gulped it down. I then fixed my hair and face and sat down on the edge of the bed.

I passed him a quick, nervous smile as he stepped into the room. He smiled back——this time there was no hint of uneasiness on his face. Instead of coming directly to the bed, he went to the switchboard and flipped a switch, engulfing the room in darkness. I felt his hands on my skin but couldn't see his face. I could only hear the collective sound of our breathing and the nervous thumping of our hearts. I did not quite understand how he managed to undress me in the dark. But then I realized I wasn't fully naked. I had my undergarments on. I felt his bare, warm skin as he lowered himself on top of me. I wanted to see how aroused he was; I wanted to see his expression while he made love to me. Having sex for the first time in complete darkness was not what I wanted. But I didn't want to complain again, so I ignored that thought and focused on what was going on between us. My body ached with desire as he started leaving a trail of kisses down my neck. I closed my eyes and grasped the bed sheet in my fists. I moaned loudly before my mind went completely blank, and I fell into a deep, dreamless sleep.

Momentary Bliss

The next morning, I woke up with a heavy head. I tried to remember what exactly had happened last night but my memory failed me. I remembered Aariz's words: 'We will make love tonight.' But I didn't feel any different. I had heard a million stories from girlfriends about losing one's virginity—about the soreness between the legs; the breaking of the hymen; the blood-stained sheets. But I didn't feel any of that; only my head throbbed with pain. As I turned around to get a glass of water, I suddenly realized that I was fully clothed. Didn't Aariz take off my clothes last night? Of course he did. I remembered that part very well. But what had happened after that? I tried to gather the pieces of last night's memory but failed. The last thing I remembered was him lying on top of me and kissing my neck. Other than that, my mind was completely blank. Why couldn't I remember anything? It was supposed to be a very special night for me. The most memorable one. Before I could get up or do anything else, I saw Aariz making his way to the room, bearing a breakfast tray.

'Hey, good morning. Thank God, you're up.' He beamed at me as he put the tray on the side table.

I smiled at him nervously.

'I contemplated waking you up but couldn't. You were sleeping like a baby. I just couldn't disturb you.' He sat down next to me, holding my hand.

'I've brought breakfast for you.'

'That's . . . very thoughtful of you.'

'Let's eat. I'm very hungry,' he said and started buttering a slice of toast.

With every passing minute, I grew more impatient. I wanted him to fill me in on the details.

'Aariz . . . did you . . . put on my clothes last night?' I asked him.

He looked at me and nodded.

'Okay,' I murmured, cursing my brain for forgetting everything.

'Why, what happened? You didn't like it?'

'No, that's not what I meant,' I told him. 'I . . . just can't remember when it happened.'

'How would you remember, Zynah? You were sound asleep by the time we finished.' He smiled.

'Right,' I nodded.

'Last night was special in so many ways,' he said and winked. 'I hope you have no doubts about my feelings any more. You know how much I love you.'

I looked up at him, into his eyes, trying to read his face.

'What happened last night?' I asked him, trying to gauge his reaction.

'What you had been waiting for,' he said and flashed me a smile.

'Did we . . . have sex?' I asked.

He nodded.

'Are you sure? Because I don't recall anything of that sort . . .'

'Zynah . . . we did have it. I enjoyed every bit of it.'

I looked at his face and thought, what a skilled liar he was. There wasn't a hint of hesitation on his face or in his eyes. I couldn't remember the intricate details of the previous night, but I knew for sure that we did not have sex. What made him lie about it? He could have told me the truth.

'What happened?' he asked, breaking my reverie.

'Uh, nothing,' I said, looking down at my plate again.

'Are you feeling okay?' he asked, concerned.

I nodded as I looked back at him.

Putting my plate on the bed, he leaned closer to me, swept my hair to one side and put his arms around my neck.

'I love you, Zynah.'

'I love you too,' I whispered, still in a trance.

What are you hiding from me, Aariz? Is there any problem you're afraid to share with me? Please, let me know if there is . . . Please. I want to know, I pleaded in my head.

Doubting the Doubts

After our so-called sexual encounter, I did see a change in Aariz's attitude towards me. He had become more attentive, caring and affectionate but we still did not have sex. He did express his love in the form of a few kisses here and there but did not initiate anything beyond that. This made me unhappy but I did not bring it up again, as I did not want to sound like a nagging wife. However, deep down I knew that things were not as transparent as they appeared. I had to know the truth. I had to unravel the mystery.

A few days later, I received a call from Soniya.

'Hey!' Soniya said.

'Hi, Sonz. How are you doing?' I asked her, sitting on my bed.

'Zee, are you free this evening?'

'Um, yeah, why?'

'Let's meet up.'

There was an urgency in her voice.

'Yeah, but can we meet tomorrow?' I asked.

'It's urgent, Zee.'

'But . . .'

'I'll wait for you at Hard Rock Café. Be there in an hour,' she said, and hung up.

Perplexed, I looked at my phone screen, wondering what could be the matter. Then put the thought away for the time being and got up to get ready. An hour later, I pushed open the heavy wooden door of the café and walked in. Sonya was seated at our usual booth, busy on her laptop.

'What's up, Sonz?' I asked, taking a seat in front of her.

'Zynah . . .' She looked up and smiled at me weakly. 'I might be wrong, but I need to show you something.'

I crossed my brows in confusion as she turned the laptop in my direction.

'Do you think this person is Aariz?' She pointed towards a picture of a group of men at a party, dancing and cheering in an inebriated state.

I narrowed my eyes and looked closely.

'Umm, yes. That's Aariz,' I finally said. 'Of course, that's him.'

'Oh-kay,' Soniya said slowly.

'But what happened?' I asked, my heartbeat quickening.

'And what about this one?' She showed me another picture where Aariz was sitting on a beach with a white guy, nuzzling his neck.

'Yes, that's Aariz,' I confirmed.

'So I was right . . .'

'What do you mean? What are you trying to say?' I asked, my voice becoming shaky.

'All I'm trying to say is . . .' Soniya said. 'Aariz has another account on Facebook which he operates under a different identity.'

'What? No way! He has only one Facebook account that he rarely uses!' I told her.

'I'll tell you why I said that. Last night, as I was going through my newsfeed, I came across a few photos of one of my Canadian ex-colleagues. Aariz's uncanny resemblance with one of the persons in the pictures made me observe them carefully. After seeing all of them, I realized that Aariz was tagged with a different name, hence a different account. Here, let me show you that account.' Soniya pulled the laptop towards her and opened the aforementioned Facebook profile. I felt the blood rush to my face.

'See this. Aariz is Aaron Kay on this other account.'

I clenched my fists under the table as I looked at the picture on the screen. She was right. It was Aariz's profile. He had put a close-up of his face as the display picture. The cover photo was him with a few other men. I looked at Sonya mockingly.

'What happened?' she asked me, confused.

'This could also be a fake profile, Soniya! What are you exactly implying?' I said, raising my voice. Why was she trying to humiliate me?

'It's not a fake profile, Zynah! Look at the comments. I have checked out all his pictures and those of people tagged here. All of them are real and are based in Canada. Wasn't Aariz also studying in Canada before he came to London?'

Irritated, I snatched the laptop out of her hands and started clicking on the pictures.

'Zee.' She placed her hand on my shoulder. 'Aariz is hiding something from you. His secret Facebook account proves that. It's time you talked to him about it. For your own sake.'

'But . . . he might be using this ID for his friends. A lot of people have two Facebook accounts—one for their family and one for friends,' I tried to reason with her.

'It's not his second account that's bothering me. It's the comments on these pictures. Such comments are shared with lovers, not friends. Is he even straight?'

I paused to look at her, my fingers trembling.

'Yes, Zynah. I doubt that he is. I haven't told you this but I did notice something odd about him at your wedding. Zynah,' she sighed, 'please listen to me carefully. You need to find out before it's too late.'

I looked back at the laptop screen, at his pictures with his male friends. In one of them, a guy was kissing Aariz on his cheek making him blush.

Maybe my friend was right. Maybe the truth had been right in front of my eyes all these days.

🎧

Aariz was already at home when I got back. He was in the washroom, taking a bath. I entered the room and slumped heavily on to the bed, the day's events whirring in my head. Suddenly, I felt something vibrate. I sat up and pulled it from under the blanket. It was Aariz's cell phone. He had put it on silent mode and hidden it under the covers. A JM was calling him. I had never heard this name before. Who was he? A colleague, a friend, or someone else? Could he be James by any chance? Or could it be the guy from Aariz's picture on the beach? I had to find out. Luckily, I had seen him enter his passcode once and remembered it. I unlocked his phone and browsed through it. I opened the call log and dialled JM's number. With my eyes on the washroom door, I tucked the phone shakily under my ear. I knew Aariz could come out any time and catch me in the act.

Suddenly someone answered. 'Aaron, where were you? Why didn't you answer my call?' a man said on the other end of the line.

I was convulsed with emotion when I heard another man address Aariz as Aaron. It proved that Aariz had two accounts on Facebook, and he had kept his other identity—Aaron—hidden from me. Despite it being cold in the room, sweat trickled down my face. I did not know what to think of this person. Who was he and what relationship did my husband have with him?

'Babe, are you there? Hello?' he asked.

I ended the call and put the phone down on the table. Right then, Aariz stepped out of the washroom. I quickly wiped off the sweat from my face and smiled.

'Hey, what's up? Where were you all day?' he asked, towelling his hair dry. When I did not say anything, he stepped closer and picked up his phone from the table.

I inspected him closely as he effortlessly swiped the screen with his fingers. He would soon find out that someone had called JM from his phone and that someone could only be me. Before he could throw questions at me, I decided it was time I bombarded him with mine.

'By the way, some JM was calling you a moment ago. I answered but he ended the call abruptly,' I said, gauging his reaction. 'I called him back but he didn't say anything.'

'Oh, JM . . .' He looked away, letting out a soft laugh. 'That's the same James from our office actually. I have saved his number as JM. You know, a nickname for James.' He shrugged coolly without looking me in the eye.

'But I have never met him before,' I said.

'Well, he works in the IT security department and our IT guys rarely step out of their cabins. They have a lot of work,' he explained.

'Right,' I said, my voice low.

I stopped myself from cross-questioning him. I could have asked him why he had a nickname for only one employee. What was so special about him? Why would an employee call him 'babe'? Why did he have two accounts on Facebook? And why had he kept the second account a secret? But I stayed quiet. I knew Aariz would brush off my concerns and make some excuse or the other if I confronted him. But what if . . . Aariz was gay?

I struggled hard to hold myself together, but I could not stop the tears from streaming down my cheeks. After all, till when could I ignore all the signs? I had to prove myself wrong. I had to know the truth. Once and for all.

The Harsh Reality

The next morning, after he had left for work, I made up my mind to spy on Aariz. I had tried hard not to dwell any further on it, but I could not stop my urge to find out what was going on. As his wife, I felt that I had the right to know about my husband's strange behaviour. For the first time since I had moved here, I looked into his closet and rummaged through the other cabinets and drawers in our room that he used. The only suspicious item appeared to be a tube of lubricant that was tucked inside one of his drawers. I inspected it and was shocked to learn that it was a lube for anal sex. Why did he have anal lube in the drawer? Did he use it the night when we first attempted to make love? As far as I knew, we did not have any sort of sexual intercourse. There had been no stains on my body or the bed sheet when I had woken up the next morning. Aariz had tried to convince me that we had made love but I know I was just playing along until now. I would have continued to believe that Aariz could never have sex, or perhaps he suffered from erectile dysfunction. But I became suspicious when I found out about his secret Facebook account.

I did not say anything to Aariz when he returned home that evening. He went about his regular routine. I wanted to go through his cell phone or laptop. Those devices could give me more insight into his secret life but he was seldom without them. I would have to wait to access his laptop when he wasn't around.

My chance came one evening when he made plans with some friends from school.

As soon as he got ready and left, I reached for his laptop and thankfully found that I did not need a password. I opened the iMessage folder and found several conversations as I scrolled down the list. The chat that piqued my interest was with JM—the same JM who had called him 'babe' over the phone.

I scrolled through the entire conversation:

Aariz: What's up? Missing me? ;)
JM: There isn't a single moment when I don't miss you, babe. You know that.
Aariz: I miss you too. Xoxo
JM: I have started missing your warmth in my bed. When are you coming over to stay for a night again? I can't wait to cuddle you.
Aariz: I'll be with you soon, love. I might drop by this evening.
JM: Let me know before coming. I want to prepare dinner for my love.
Aariz: Sure. Xoxo

Tears stung my eyes. One of the pictures in their chat was the same as the one I'd seen on his Facebook profile—a photo of Aariz on the beach. Someone else had taken the photo and clearly that someone was James because he had sent it to Aariz. My eyes began to swim and my body went limp but I continued to look through his files and folders. I browsed through the pictures saved on his laptop and then scanned the 'history' of the web browser. I couldn't believe what I had just seen and read. I put my elbows on the laptop, folded my hands together and inhaled deeply, trying to calm myself.

I had been so blinded by my own love that I had not noticed his lack of passion for me. So enamoured was I that I had not even considered whether he was heterosexual or not. I did not know what made me believe that he was interested in me. Why had I thought that he wanted to marry me as much as I did? I should have known that he wasn't into me when he had rejected the idea of marriage in the beginning. I had been a fool to pressure him into a relationship; forced relationships don't work and this one wouldn't either. I shut my eyes and let out a loud sob—a final and complete admission that my husband was gay.

The Confession

I was still in front of Aariz's computer, with my head bowed down, when the door of my room creaked open. I looked up to find Aariz standing in front of me.

'Zynah . . .' he began but his voice trailed off as his eyes fell on his laptop and then back at me. 'What are you doing?' he asked in a low voice.

I turned the laptop screen to face him. A look of horror crossed Aariz's face when he saw the photograph of him and James canoodling on the beach staring back at him.

'Oh, that's . . . James,' he said, trying to act as if everything were normal. 'I almost forgot to tell you that both of us studied in the same college in Canada. We're very good friends.'

I clenched my fists underneath the table as I mustered the courage to confront him.

'James is your boyfriend, isn't he?' I asked him, my eyes not leaving his. Every nerve in my body shook with agony.

'What?' he asked, in a startled whisper, pretending that he couldn't believe what I had just asked.

'I asked a simple question, Aariz,' I repeated, my heart thumping loudly. 'Is James your boyfriend?'

'What are you trying to say?' he said, and shook his head. 'Of course, he is my good friend. A good boyfriend.' He shrugged, again trying to act cool. But he didn't look convincing. He knew something was wrong. He knew that I had found out.

'Stop lying, I know everything. I've found out about you.' My voice broke. Suddenly, I realized that I had no energy to utter another word. My entire body throbbed with pain.

'Found out what?' he whispered, his expression guarded.

'That you're gay!' I screamed at the top of my lungs, shoving away the laptop. The outburst surprised both Aariz and me.

'Zynah . . .,' he said and took a step towards me, his eyes filling with tears.

'Go away, Aariz! You fucking ruined my life . . .'

Tears endlessly streamed down my cheeks as I shoved him away.

'Listen to me, Zynah.'

He tried to embrace me.

'Why should I listen to you? You kept a secret from me, from my family. You could have told me everything about yourself. I would have walked away. Why did you marry me, Aariz? Why did you ruin my life? Answer me!'

'Zynah, please calm down.'

He held my arm but I shoved him away.

'No! Leave me alone! I don't want to be with you!'

Aariz continued to hold my shoulders in a firm grip.

'Leave me, Aariz!'

I tried to struggle out of his grip but it was much stronger than I'd imagined.

'Just listen to me, please! Once!'

Aariz engulfed me in his warm, soothing arms and I gave up the struggle. He stroked my hair gently with his fingers and kissed the top of my head. Shivers ran down my spine when he kissed me and I began to cry again. I brought my palms up and sobbed into my hands.

Aariz went down on his knees in front of me and took my hands in his. I shivered but he calmed me down by stroking my hand.

'What you've found out about me is . . . true. It's all true.'

He looked at me, the fear had left his eyes.

'I'm a homosexual . . . have been a homosexual for as long as I can remember.' His fingers softly interlaced with mine as he declared it.

I freed one of my hands from his grip and clamped it against my mouth to hold back the sobs.

'When I was in Canada, living on my own, everything seemed perfect and normal. I have been in a steady relationship with James since my high school years.'

I cringed when he said that.

Aariz continued undeterred. 'But things turned bad when I moved back to London to look after the family business. I had to leave James behind. We tried a long-distance relationship but when we realized we couldn't work it, I asked him to relocate to the UK and he readily agreed. I offered him employment at our company so that he could be close to me.'

I wiped off the tears, trying hard to listen to him though I was shattered from the inside.

'I managed to set up a smooth life for James and me but it didn't last long. Soon, Mom started to ask if I had a girlfriend because she wanted me to get married. When I told her that I had no such person in my life, she demanded that I meet prospective fiancées. I would reject them, saying I did not like any of them. But then, you came into the picture.'

I held my breath as he looked back into my eyes.

'Seeing your interest in me, Mom and Dad told me to get to know you better by spending more time with you. I couldn't make any excuses this time. And I also couldn't tell my parents about my real identity. However, one day, I did gather some courage to speak to Mom about it. When I told her I wasn't interested in women, she thought I was joking. She said I'd start taking interest once I was married. Before I could explain myself to her, she walked away. Telling Dad that I was not interested in women but men would have left him baffled, hurt. He would have never accepted me or my partner. Dad belongs to an honourable family and has a solid reputation here. He's known for running a leading design company in London. Had I admitted my sexuality to him, Dad would have been devastated. Both Mom and Dad. I could have lost them forever. Or quite possibly, they would have disowned me. So, for the sake of my parent's reputation, to save myself from the taunts of relatives and friends, I married you, thinking I would get away from the societal pressure and lead a so-called normal life.' He let out a small laugh.

I let out a gasp of distress, not knowing how long I had been holding my breath. Every word coming out of his mouth was like a sharp shard.

'I knew from the beginning that it would be impossible to make you believe that I am straight, but I kept dragging

the matter as long as I could. But . . . then something
unexpected happened. I developed feelings for you. I felt
attracted to you.'

I looked at his distraught face, my eyes softening.

'It's true that I have only loved James all my life . . .
but since *we* got married and became close, I started
feeling something for you.'

I furrowed my brows, trying to understand what he
was saying.

'What . . . do you mean?' I mumbled.

'I don't know what it means but it's true. I have
feelings for you, Zynah. I don't know what to make of
them but they're here,' he said, pointing to his chest.
'These feelings for you are true.'

I stared at him in sheer confusion. Taking advantage
of my reaction, he pulled me closer and wrapped his arms
around my neck.

'Zynah, I love you. You're the only woman I've ever
loved. I did not know I could ever love a woman until I
met you and married you. I do not even know what this
means. I do not know if it makes me a bisexual, but the
truth is I love you and I do not want you to leave me.
Ever. Please.' All of a sudden, he broke into tears, leaving
me breathless. I felt empty inside.

'Aariz . . .' I whispered.

'Zynah.' He moved back, looking at my face. 'Let's
give our relationship another chance.' He cupped my face
in his hands. 'I don't know if I will ever be able to change
but I want to give it a try. I want to lead a happy married
life with you. Just give me another chance. I can't do this
alone. I need you to help me fix everything. Say you will
help me? Please, Zynah?' More tears rushed out of his
eyes as he held my hands in his.

I'd never seen him in this state. So weak. So vulnerable. This was not the Aariz I knew. He was charming, sophisticated, slightly snobbish, but never an emotional wreck.

'Zynah, I know I've ruined your life by keeping you in the dark. I don't have the right to ruin anybody's life just to conceal my real identity from the world but trust me when I say this. With you I realized I could see myself as a different person, be a different person.'

Mustering the courage, I took his hands in mine and looked into his eyes.

'Aariz, this is not you,' I whispered. 'Do not become someone you're not. You cannot change yourself for me.'

'But I can try, right?' he smiled weakly. 'Your love might change me.'

I looked away, contemplating what he had said. Would giving him another chance solve our problems? Would that make him love me? Would he be exclusively mine or remain divided between two individuals? But how would he suddenly become straight? Was that even possible? I did not understand what to make of all this. Everything seemed jumbled up. On the one hand, he had come out, but on the other, he wanted to stay with me. How could he do that? Did he not have enough courage to talk to his parents about himself? Did he want me to help him out? The deafening sound of my heartbeat echoed in my ears as I looked at his face, filled with desolation and helplessness.

The next day, before leaving for work, Aariz came up to me and apologized again. Without giving him an answer,

I turned my back on him. He patted me on my shoulder, heaved a sigh, and then walked away.

I couldn't believe that Aunty Raima had been oblivious to Aariz's sexuality all her life. She was his mother. Mothers know everything about their children. Nothing is hidden from them. During breakfast, I decided to ask her about Aariz.

'Mom . . . I need to talk to you . . .' I told her, my voice guarded.

'Sure, honey. Go ahead.'

'I wanted to talk about Aariz.'

Her soft expression suddenly turned grave. 'What about him?'

'Did you know that Aariz is . . . homosexual?' I said.

'What . . .?' she frowned. 'What are you saying? Have you gone . . .'

'Mom . . . please,' I interrupted her. 'I confronted him and he accepted it.'

'What?' she whispered as she clamped a hand over her mouth, stunned.

'Did you know about this?' I asked her.

'Honey . . . I . . . I don't even know what that really means . . .'

'Mom . . .' I held her hand. 'Please tell me.'

A tear escaped her eye as she said, 'He once told me he wasn't into women. He told me he wouldn't marry you or any other girl, but I refused to listen to him. I did not let him explain. Even if he felt something for the same sex, I was sure it was only temporary. I wanted him to marry a woman so he could understand what a real relationship is. I told him his perspective would change once he married you.'

I looked away, listening to her.

'And believe me, Zynah, I do believe he has changed. He loves you so much.'

I sniffed, a tear escaping my eye.

'I know he loves you as much as you love him. That's why you guys got married, right? Zynah, my child,' Aunty Raima said, as she held my chin, 'Do not think otherwise. I suggest you start a family with him. Have a child. That is the only way to keep him under your control.'

Her advice startled me.

'But, Mom ... I ...'

'Think about it, Zynah.'

I looked at her, considering what she'd said.

Would a child really change Aariz? Would having a family make him completely mine? I did not want to doubt Aariz's feelings for me. If he said he loved me, then maybe he did. He confided in me and told me everything irrespective of the fact that I could tell his family and mine. Wasn't that enough to prove his love for me? And being his wife, shouldn't I help him out? What could go wrong if I helped him? I should do everything to save my marriage. Nobody could stop me now.

PART FOUR

Rehaan

'I will stop you,' I declared, after hearing her heart-wrenching tale.

Leaning over the deck of the Tower Bridge, she shot me a sceptical look. 'What do you mean?' she asked, baffled.

'What do you think you're doing, Zynah? Do you think that you are doing yourself or him a favour by continuing this charade? Do you think you can be happy with him? Maybe you've no idea, but you're walking down a path to self-destruction.'

She looked away, shrugging dismissively.

'Believing that your gay husband would somehow magically turn into a straight, loving husband is downright stupid.'

She sighed, closing her eyes.

'I know a lot of gay men. They never become straight. They stay the way they are. All their lives. Your so-called mother-in-law is just fooling you. She doesn't want you to leave her son.'

She opened her eyes and looked at me.

'You know you're walking down the wrong path. You know you're chasing an impossible dream. Why not just leave him for his own good? For *your* own good?' I asked.

'He says he loves me and wants to be with me,' she said, trying to convince herself.

'That's utter bullshit!' I said, my face expressionless. 'He doesn't love you, Zynah. He only loves himself. He's manipulating you so that you don't leave him. And not because he loves you. He is doing this because he wants to keep up this pretence for the sake of his family, the society. He married you to conform to social norms. He's a coward who does not have the courage to face his own reality! Can't you see that?'

'That's not the point.'

'Then what's the damn point?' I asked, irritated at her idiocy.

'The point is . . .' She turned her face towards me. 'I *love* him. Despite the fact that he doesn't love me, or he is gay, I love him. And you don't leave the people you love. You stay with them. Do you get it now? I can't leave him. I just can't.' She shook her head lightly.

'You only *think* that you love him. The truth is you stopped loving him the day you found out he was gay.'

'That's not true!' she shot back. 'My love is not bound to his sexuality. Never was. I love him for the person he is.'

'Zynah, you can fool me but you can't fool yourself. At least be true to your own damn self.'

'Go away, Rehaan! I was wrong to assume that you had changed. You're as stubborn as ever! I made a mistake coming down here with you!' she screamed, pushing me away.

'I am stubborn? It's you who's stubborn! I don't understand how you continue being so stubborn, so blind, so brainless! He's gay, Zynah. He won't love you the way you want him to! Dammit, he would never even make love to you!'

'Shut up! You have no right to comment on my personal life!' She glowered at me, blinking rapidly. I couldn't ignore the tears in her eyes.

'Why not? Tell me, did he have sex with you?' I asked bluntly.

'That's none of your business!'

'Oh yes, it is very much my business. So, tell me. Did he have sex with you? How are you going to bear his child if he doesn't even touch you?'

'Fuck off, Rehaan!' she yelled, walking away. But I didn't let her. I grabbed her by her waist and made her face me.

'I know you're lying, Zynah,' I whispered. 'Stop defending him.'

For a moment, we locked eyes with each other. I could see the pain in them. She wasn't happy in this relationship. I could clearly see she was lying, trying to protect her failing marriage. Before I could wrap her in my arms and comfort her, she squirmed in an attempt to get out of my grip.

'I've had sex with him, and it was very satisfying,' she said, enunciating every word so I could hear it clearly.

Damn it! Another lie.

'You know what?' I whispered back, 'you've lost it, Zynah. Completely lost it . . .'

Before I could utter another word, she raised her hand as if to slap me but didn't. I straightened my shirt and looked up but she had already turned to leave. I didn't try to stop her. Without another word, she walked away, leaving me behind with my misery.

Zynah

When I told Soniya everything about Aariz the next day and asked her for her advice, she laughed and called me foolish. She wanted me to immediately get a divorce and start over. But she didn't try to understand my situation, my feelings. It was easier to say such things. Until now, I was dealing with only her accusations, but now Rehaan had also jumped on the bandwagon. But his argument was different from Soniya's. He saw this as an opportunity to whisk me away. He was in love with me and instead of understanding my feelings for Aariz, he wanted to poison my mind against him, so that I would choose him over my husband. After our recent meeting, I realized I had made a mistake by telling him everything. This had only made my life more complicated.

I tried to change the subject and told Soniya what had happened with Rehaan the previous day.

'What are you saying? You've told him everything?' Soniya asked.

'I thought he'd be mature about it and offer some solid advice but I was wrong. He's still the same . . .' I said, looking away.

'Zynah, what else did you expect from him? Any sane person would give you the same advice. I am quite sure your support group members also tell you the same thing.'

I didn't try to defend my situation because I knew she was right. In the sessions too, I had been advised to call it quits and move out.

'Whatever. I have already made a fool of myself. I'm never seeing him again.'

'Aariz?' Soniya raised her brows.

'No!' I glowered. 'I'm talking about Rehaan!'

'Yeah, right,' she mumbled.

'I guess you shouldn't have tried to slap him, Zynah,' she said after a minute of silence. 'The poor guy deserves better.'

In the next instant, my phone rang. I looked at it and was surprised to see Rehaan's picture flashing on it. It was a Facebook Messenger call. I had no idea that you could call someone even if you were not friends with them on the social media website.

'Hello?' I said, my voice low, indifferent.

'Hi Zynah, it's me Rehaan.'

'I know it's you, Rehaan,' I said, looking at Soniya.

'Listen, I called to apologize. I, uh . . . I shouldn't have said all that. My behaviour was out of line . . . I was being mean and judgmental. I'm really sorry for everything.'

I did not realize that I had held my breath throughout his monologue.

'And, by everything, I mean everything, Zynah. I am sorry for hurting you. Back then . . . and even now.'

Soniya shot me a confused look when I didn't respond.

'Zynah, are you there?' Rehaan asked.

'Yes, I'm here,' I replied, my throat constricting.

'So, have you . . . forgiven me?'

'It's okay, Rehaan. Maybe it's not entirely your fault. I shouldn't have tried to slap you. I'm sorry,' I said. Soniya passed me a reassuring look.

'Let's just put it behind us,' he said, his voice relaxing. 'Anyway, are you free this evening? Can we meet?'

'Meet?' I asked, as I raised a brow and looked at Soniya.

She gave me a positive nod and mouthed the words 'say yes'.

'Yeah, only if you're free?' he asked, waiting for my reply.

'Um, okay,' I said.

'Great! I'll wait for you at the same music store at 5. See you then?'

'Okay, see you.' I hung up and looked at her, my face serious.

'What?' she asked.

'Why did you make me say yes?'

'Zynah, stop blaming me. You wanted to say yes so you said it. What's wrong in catching up with old friends?'

I looked way, sighing.

'He realized he acted like a jerk last night and apologized. And trust me, it takes a lot of guts to apologize to someone when you know you aren't wrong. You're just lucky to have a friend like him.'

'What do you mean?'

'You know what I mean. Besides, I'm getting late for work. Need to go. I'll call you at night for the deets!' Grabbing her stuff from the coffee table, she quickly patted me on my shoulder and left.

Going back to Rough Trade, my favourite music store, was like taking a walk down memory lane. This used to be my favourite haunt before I got married. My eyes became moist when I thought about those good old days—glorious and carefree. I had Rehaan to thank for bringing back the happy memories.

'I almost thought you wouldn't come,' he said as I walked towards him.

'Umm . . .' I hesitated, not knowing what to say. 'Did you buy anything?' I asked, changing the subject.

'Yeah, I picked up two,' he said, handing the music albums to me.

'I didn't know you were into pop music,' I mumbled.

'Well, I'm into everything, you know. Pop. Rock. Jazz.' He smiled, his cheeks turning pink. 'I am glad we still have these stores around. Nothing beats the joy of listening to good old vinyl records.'

'Right,' I said, suppressing a smile.

'Should we go out for coffee or do you want to hang around here for a bit?' he asked.

'No, no. I think we should leave.'

'Sure.'

Across the street, we found a small, cosy coffee shop. Rehaan said it was quite popular with the hipsters. We placed our order and settled down at a corner table. An uncomfortable silence engulfed us as we waited for our cups of coffee. Our eyes locked every now and then but neither of us initiated a conversation.

'So . . .' Rehaan finally spoke. 'How's everyone at home? Who else is there besides Aariz?'

I tried to gauge his expression. I didn't want to get into another argument about my husband. But he seemed to be in a good mood and the question seemed pretty harmless.

'There's Aariz and his parents, Aunty Raima and Uncle Kamran.'

'Are they good to you?' He raised a brow.

'Of course, they're my family.'

'That's good to know.' He nodded, biting his lower lip.

'What about you? Where are you staying in London? Same place with that Indian flatmate?' I asked, taking my cup from the waiter and placing it on the table.

'No . . . financially, I am in a much better place. I have my own apartment now, on mortgage of course,' he said matter-of-factly.

'Oh,' I said, taking a sip of the sweet liquid.

'By doing a full-time job after my masters, driving Uber on weekends and taking up a few photography courses, I managed to save some money and eventually opened my own photography studio here.'

'Doesn't your studio reap good profits? I mean, why do you need to drive a taxi when you have your own setup?'

'I don't do it for money. I drive for myself, to calm my senses. It gives me time to think.'

'Makes sense. I'm glad you've achieved what you wanted to.'

'Not yet. I am not even close.'

'What?' I exclaimed. 'You have your *own* photography studio and your *own* apartment. You earn good money. You are your own boss. What else do you need?'

'I am still looking for my soulmate.'

'What? That sounds poetic.' I shook my head.

'Poetic and spiritual. You know what?' he said, leaning forward. 'I have always believed in this quote by Rumi, "What you seek is seeking you. It's nice to think that what you love actually loves you, what you desire desires you, and what you want wants you.'"

'So, who wants to be with you?' I asked, suddenly getting intrigued by this conversation. 'Is there someone in your life?'

'If I'm not wrong, you're trying to find out about my relationship status.'

'Of course, I am. What's wrong with that?'

'No. There is nothing wrong with that.'

'So, is there someone?' I asked, trying very hard not to sound too desperate. Deep down, I really wanted to know whether he was single or not.

'I've met a lot of girls here. Thanks to Tinder. But I'm not dating anyone right now.'

'So, you're single then?'

'For now, yes.'

'Don't tell me your Amma hasn't already found a girl for you in Lahore.'

'Well, yes, she has. She keeps trying,' he said, smiling. 'But I haven't said yes to any of them.'

'*Chalo, koi na koi mil jayegi* [You will eventually find someone]. Wait for the right time.'

'Or maybe, I should wait for the right person?' he asked, his eyes locked with mine.

'Yeah, maybe,' I said, breaking our gaze.

Rehaan

After our little coffee date, we strolled down the street aimlessly. I felt the crisp December air on my face and shivered slightly.

'Does Aariz know you are here with me?' I suddenly asked her, forgetting that this was a touchy topic.

'Yes, I have told him. He's not in town though. He'll return from Chicago next week,' she said, her voice composed.

'Does he know about me?' I asked, giving her a sidelong glance.

She looked at me and nodded.

'Does he approve of you meeting your male friends?'

'What's wrong with that?'

'Most husbands are possessive, you know. But hey, you don't have to worry. Aariz can't be possessive about you. He clearly isn't the jealous type.' I chuckled, hoping she would ignore my sarcasm.

'He trusts me,' she snapped back.

'Of course he does. You're not the one who's cheating on him.'

She stopped in her tracks as soon as these words came out of my mouth. I had done it again. I just couldn't help taking digs at her husband. She gave me a cold stare.

'Oh, c'mon,' I said, raising my hands in surrender. 'I was just . . . kidding.'

She looked upset.

'Zynah, don't tell me you can't even take my jokes now?'

'If my relationship with my husband is a joke to you . . . then I don't even know what to say,' she said, her voice breaking. I didn't want to spoil her mood or our evening.

'Okay, fine,' I sighed. 'I'm sorry.'

Ignoring my hollow apology, she strode ahead, towards the Tube station.

'Acha, listen . . .' I followed her. 'Don't act like a stubborn child now. You know we're friends. *Doston mein sab chalta hai* [These things keep happening between friends].'

'Whatever, Rehaan,' she said, slowing down.

'So, when does your curfew end? How much time do you have?'

'Why?'

'I wanted to show you around, you know.' I shrugged.

'What?' She guffawed. 'You want to show me my own city? Don't you remember? I was the one who showed you around in the first place.'

I was glad she remembered our time together. It brought an instant smile to my face.

'Do you think that's London? Those touristy spots?' I said, shaking my head.

'What do you mean?' She folded her arms.

'Darling, I'll show you the real London. The city you haven't seen yet.'

'Oh, c'mon. I know this place like the back of my hand. Every nook and cranny. There's not even a single place I haven't visited,' she said.

'Are you challenging me, Zynah Malik?'

'Yes, I am, Rehaan Sheikh!'

Zynah

Surprisingly, it was easy to convince Aunty Raima about my upcoming plan with Rehaan. When I told her a friend had moved to the city and had requested me to show him around, she thought it was a good idea. She wanted me to go out as much as possible, especially when Aariz was not in town. If only I could tell her what real solitude was. If only I could tell her how isolated I felt even in Aariz's presence.

🎧

I spotted Rehaan sitting on a bench outside St Pancras Old Church as I parked my car. He had asked me to meet him here. I wondered why. Was he trying to make me revisit our memories? Or was he trying to make me understand that I had a life outside my relationship with Aariz?

'Hey,' I said, making my way to the bench.

'Hey,' he said, looking up. 'What's up?'

I noticed the camera strapped across his chest.

'Why did you call me here?' I asked him. 'I have been here a million times,' I reminded him.

'I thought you liked this place.'

'I still do.'

'So why did you stop coming?'

'I never said that,' I retorted.

'Really?' He pondered over my statement for a bit and then said, 'I think you did mention yesterday that after marriage you stopped visiting the places you loved.'

'I don't remember saying that.' I turned away, looking at the main entrance of the church, trying to change the topic. 'Anyway, are we here to visit this church? You couldn't come up with anything better?' I smiled at him, folding my arms. 'Why do I have a feeling that you're going to fail this challenge?' I asked him.

'I won't.'

He stood across me, adjusting the collar of his black sweatshirt. Maybe I hadn't noticed before but he looked different; he looked handsome. Even his hairstyle had changed over the years. And the beard really suited his boyish face.

He suddenly looked up and our eyes met. He had caught me staring at him.

'Hello? Where are you lost?' he asked, snapping his fingers to get my attention.

'Um, nothing.'

'So, ready for the challenge?'

'Yes,' I said with a nod.

🎧

'Where are you going?' Rehaan inquired.

'I thought we were going around the city?' I said as I unlocked my car.

'Yes, we are, but not in our cars.'

'Why not?' I asked, confused.

'Well.' He took a few steps in my direction. 'Our first activity involves seeing the city on . . . bicycles.'

'What?' I frowned. 'Are you serious?'

'Yes.'

'You can't be! I don't have a bicycle.'

'Don't worry about that. I have hired them,' he said and started walking in the opposite direction. I followed him and soon saw two bicycles parked against the wall.

'Rehaan,' I said, shaking my head. 'We can't roam around on bicycles. That's so silly,' I insisted, waving my hands.

'No, it's not. It's a lot of fun! You took me around on a tour bus. Did I complain? No! Now you have to do as I say. C'mon. Give it a try!'

For a moment I stared at the bike. No matter what he said, it still seemed like a stupid idea.

'Zynah! What are you thinking? Trust me. You'll love it, I'm telling you. Don't you trust me?'

'Um . . .'

'I'm not asking you to jump off a cliff. C'mon. It's only a bike!'

'What if . . . what if I fall?'

'Is that what you're afraid of?'

I nodded sheepishly.

'You won't. I am here,' he assured me.

I locked my eyes with his, my heart racing.

'Plus, I've got us helmets. So there is nothing to worry about.' He disengaged the helmet from the bike's handle and handed it to me. 'Take it.'

Leaving my hesitation and fear behind, I stepped forward, taking the helmet from his hand. He passed me a victorious smile in return. I wore the helmet gingerly and then mounted the bike, my legs shaking. I had not ridden one in ages.

'On your marks, get set, go!' He pedalled towards the main road. I imitated him. I held the handlebar firmly and pushed the pedal, slowly gaining pace. I couldn't believe I still remembered how to ride. Feeling exhilarated, I smiled as the air rushed past my face. Rehaan slowed down to match my speed. I looked at him and suddenly both of us burst out laughing. He was right. This was truly amazing. I saw the city from a fresh perspective that day.

The sun felt good on my skin. It warmed my heart and for a second, I forgot all my problems. I was finally living in the moment. I looked around at the lush greenery, the quaint cafes lining the street, the people out on their evening walk, and then I looked at Rehaan. He was gesturing at me to take a right turn ahead. I squinted at him against the bright light. And then it happened. I lost my balance. I tried to steady myself but couldn't and let out a loud scream. Rehaan came running and broke my fall just in time. Blood rushed to my cheeks as he wrapped his strong arms around my waist. He smiled at me reassuringly, making my heart skip a beat.

On our way home, he asked me if I would meet him the next day for another adventure. I instantly said yes. Visiting these places with him was just an excuse. What I was most excited about was meeting him every day. I felt happier in his presence. He had come into my life once again like a breath of fresh air.

🎧

The next day, I met him directly at Regent's Canal. He looked really cute in a pair of shorts and a striped cotton shirt. I let out a giggle as he walked towards me. He thought I was making fun of him and seemed offended. But then he too burst out laughing. I was glad we had restored the camaraderie in our relationship.

'Remember you had told me that the church was your go-to place whenever you wanted some peace of mind?' he asked.

'Yes,' I said.

'Well, this is my church,' he declared.

'This is beautiful,' I said, soaking up the sun.

'But this is only twenty per cent of the adventure this place offers.'

'What do you mean?' I asked, confused.

'Follow me.' His face broke into a smile.

After talking to a local for a few minutes, he asked me to follow him further. Soon a kayak came into view, bobbing up and down.

'Rehaan, what's this?' I asked.

'It's a kayak. Come, let's go.' He took my hand and made me step down the dock and then into the kayak. It was a two-seater and we managed to board it quite easily without it keeling over. The local with whom Rehaan was talking earlier handed us two paddles. He smiled, wished us a wonderful ride and made his way back to the dock. Both the seats faced the same direction and, seated in the rear, I couldn't see Rehaan's face as his back was towards me.

'Rehaan, what am I supposed to do with this?' I asked, looking at the double-bladed paddle in my hands. 'I can't even hold it properly.'

'Paddling is super easy, Zynah. Just use it to propel the boat forward. I'll start doing it so you can learn from me. All right?'

With his legs stretched out in front, Rehaan started to paddle with strong strokes. He used his torso and his shoulders to rotate the paddle so that while one blade pushed back the water, the other was in the air and moving forward to take the next stroke. Rehaan slipped into a rhythm and I imitated his technique. The tandem effort propelled the kayak in a straight line through the canal.

'Got it?' Rehaan asked, looking over his shoulder so I could hear him.

'Yes,' I nodded enthusiastically, feeling an adrenaline rush.

I had never experienced this thrill before: neither with my friends, nor alone. I cursed myself for not having tried it earlier. This was a unique view of London from its canals—a perspective I would never have experienced otherwise.

🎧

We took the Tube home. It was Rehaan's idea. I got a seat but Rehaan had to stand throughout the twenty-minute journey.

'Are you okay?' I asked him.

'Yes,' he said and then realized I was rubbing my arms. 'Are *you* okay?'

I nodded.

'But you don't seem okay,' he said, scrutinizing my face. 'Are you hurt?'

How did he know that my arms hurt because of kayaking all day?

'How do you know?' I asked, surprised.

'Know what?' he asked.

'Uh, nothing,' I said, looking out of the window.

'I can read your face, Zynah,' he said.

I looked down at my hands, my heart thudding in my chest.

'I know what's on your mind. I can feel it. Maybe you are hurting here too,' he said, placing a hand on his chest.

I glared at him, and before I could launch a counter-attack, he changed the subject. 'Get a hot compress as soon as you reach home.'

Pursing my lips, I sat back and heaved a sigh, considering what he'd just said. He was right. It was my heart that hurt the most. But then what is love without the pain?

Rehaan

The next day, I wrapped up my assignments by 4 p.m. and then called Zynah and asked her to meet me at Hampstead Heath. She seemed reluctant as she had been to the park many times before but when I promised it would be a completely new experience, she agreed.

'What's up, Captain?' she asked, removing her shades. 'Enjoying the sunny afternoon?'

I smiled on hearing her call me 'Captain.' It meant we were slowly getting back on track.

'Kind of,' I said, smiling. 'How's your arm now?'

'Much better.'

'Did the compress help?'

'Yes.' She smiled, caressing her arm. 'You should have told me you were planning a picnic. I would have got a lunch basket for us.'

'Don't worry. I've already got it.' I winked at her.

'Really?' She looked surprised.

I nodded.

'But I'm not hungry right now. Are you?' she asked.

'Nope.'

'Great.' She smiled. 'So, what is the plan? Sit and chat?'

'No. We swim today.'

'What?' She looked baffled.

I nodded.

'No way.' She shook her head slowly.

'Zynah, have you ever swum in the Hampstead ponds?'

'Never. I'm not crazy.'

'But I am. Watch me do it.' I winked at her again, unbuttoning my jacket.

'Rehaan, are you crazy? The weather might seem sunny right now but soon it will get chilly. You'll end up catching a cold!' she cried.

'Don't worry, Zynah. I have done this many times. Even in winter.' By now, I had stripped down to my vest and boxers. Crossing the Mixed Bathing Pond entrance, I sprinted towards the water and jumped in with a loud splash.

'Rehaan!' Zynah shrieked.

I pushed myself up and waved at her enthusiastically, my hair sticking to my forehead.

'I'm here. I'm fine!' I assured her, smiling.

'I can't believe you! Idiot! I thought you had drowned!' She heaved a sigh of relief, clamping a hand over her mouth.

'Don't worry. I won't leave you. Not yet.' I held her gaze.

She first glared at me and then flashed one of her winning smiles. Returning the smile, I swam further away from her, relishing the cold water.

🎧

As the sky dusked, the air became cooler, making me shiver. Crossing my legs, I sat down on the damp grass along with Zynah, and enjoyed the perfect sunset in front of us.

'Rehaan, when did you get time to explore all these beautiful places?' she asked, breaking the silence.

'Well, somewhere between learning photography, buying an apartment, opening a studio and acquiring a driving license. Nothing happens overnight.'

'I'm so proud of your achievements, Rehaan. Your family must be proud too,' she continued, smiling.

'Yes, they are,' I said, unzipping my bag and taking out a pack of cigarettes. 'I'm also planning to have a photo exhibition soon,' I said, putting a cigarette between my lips. 'Want one?'

'No, thanks. But best of luck for the exhibition.' She smiled.

'You don't smoke now?' I asked.

'I quit after I got married.'

I nodded, breaking eye contact with her, and wondered what else she had given up for the sake of marriage.

'But I can see you have started smoking,' she said, raising a brow.

'Oh, this.' I took the cigarette out of my mouth and threw it away. 'Just sometimes.' I shrugged.

'Hmmm. So, Mr Rehaan Sheikh!' She turned to look at me. 'Now that you have achieved what you wanted to, I think you should get married.'

'What?' I exclaimed, looking away.

'Yes!'

'You won't believe it but Amma sent me a couple of pictures on WhatsApp this morning. She wants me to select one.'

'Really?' she asked, her cheeks turning red with excitement. 'Show them to me now!'

'Are you sure?' I asked, squinting my eyes.

'Why? Are they that bad?'

'No, I don't know. I haven't seen them yet.'

'Let me see them!'

'Wait.' I unlocked my phone and handed it to her. 'Here you go. Swipe left and choose the best one for me.'

Our hands touched as she took the phone from me, giving me butterflies in my stomach. She still had that effect on me. Blissfully unaware of the storm that raged inside me, she observed each picture with utmost attention. I looked away, my breath quickening.

'I like this girl,' she said, unconsciously putting a hand on my shoulder. 'I think she's cute. See?' She flashed the picture in front of me but I couldn't look at it. I had eyes only for her.

'See? She's cute, right?' she asked as she shifted her eyes from the phone screen to me. I caught her gaze for a moment but did not answer her question.

'Rehaan?' she asked, her voice faltering, smile fading. 'Do you like this girl?'

Without averting my eyes, I slowly nodded.

'I really like her,' I admitted almost in a whisper, my eyes locked with hers.

She looked at me uncomfortably as it became clear that I was referring to her instead of the girl in the picture. I did not know how to control my emotions. My feelings for her were transparent.

She gulped, hesitating, and then looked away, breaking the eye contact. My attempt at making her realize which girl I was talking about seemed successful.

'I think we should leave now. Here, take your phone back.' She put the phone on the grass and stood up.

We gathered our things and slowly walked out of the park. The atmosphere was fraught with tension and a daunting silence ensued.

'Can I drop you home tonight?' I asked her.

'I can just call a taxi.'

'Captain at your service, madam,' I said, smiling.

She smiled back at me, casting her eyes down.

The previous camaraderie died down as soon as we sat in the car and neither of us spoke till we reached her house. I also realized this was the first time I was dropping her off at her in-laws'. I'd not seen her house since we started hanging out again.

I slowed down the car as we reached Mallord Street.

'Yeah, that's my house,' she said, pointing at a bungalow.

'Wow, it's beautiful,' I said, bringing the car to a halt.

I got out of the car and took in the serenity of the neighbourhood. It was all calm and quiet. Peaceful.

'Humph. Money speaks for itself,' I commented.

'Thanks for the ride, Captain. Your fare?' She grinned.

'A smile would do,' I said, looking at her intently.

'See you, Rehaan,' she smiled and turned around to walk away.

'Zynah,' I called out. She turned to look at me.

'There's only one place left that I'd like you to see,' I told her.

'Oh, great,' she said.

'But there might be a problem.'

'Problem?' Her frown deepened.

'This place can be seen only at night.'

'Night? What time?'

'Around 8 or 9. Will you be able to make it?' I asked.

Before she could respond, someone called out her name.

I cocked my head slightly to see who it was. Aariz.

Zynah turned around to look at her husband.

'Aariz . . .' she said. 'You're here! When did you come?'

'I reached half an hour ago,' he said, as he stepped down from the porch. 'Thought I'd surprise you.' He reached for her hands and leaned closer until his lips found hers. He kissed her in front of me. I was devastated. Every cell in my body, every vein, my heartbeat, my breath, my entire existence burnt to ashes. I looked away, tears filling my eyes. What the hell was I doing here? I must leave as soon as possible and never come back.

'Did you miss me?' I heard Aariz ask her.

'Um . . . yes,' Zynah told him. 'Aariz, I want you to meet someone. Rehaan!' she called out.

Heartbroken, I turned to look at them, my eyes moist.

'Aariz, remember I told you about my school friend, Rehaan?' Zynah said, as Aariz wrapped his arm around her waist.

'Hi, Rehaan. Nice to meet you.'

'Nice to meet you too,' I said.

'Zynah, you should invite Rehaan over for dinner some time.'

'I will,' Zynah said as she looked at me, nodding unconsciously.

'I have an urgent call to make. You coming?' he asked her. She nodded.

'Great. See you soon, Rehaan!' He waved at me and then walked back into the house.

Without uttering a single word or bidding her goodbye, I turned away and headed back to the car. I couldn't bear to stand with her and allow her to judge my reaction because all I felt was envy.

'Rehaan!' Zynah called out but I didn't stop. 'I'll be ready at 8 p.m. tomorrow. Just text me the place. I'll be there,' she said.

I walked away, without looking back.

Zynah

I was surprised to see Aariz back from his trip so soon. My in-laws were happy to see him but I didn't share their enthusiasm. I had even forgotten for how many days he had gone or the date of his return.

My mind wandered to the last few days and the person who had kept me so busy that I had forgotten about Aariz and our strained relationship. He had opened a whole new world for me that I didn't even know existed. He had again pulled me out of the dark abyss I had fallen into and made me realize that there was still hope. I had found solace and comfort in his company. Our time together was an escape from reality, our conversations a much-needed release. He made me realize how important self-worth was. Our little adventures around the city had brought us closer. With Rehaan, I was the same old Zynah again—the girl who knew how to live life to the fullest.

I stirred my tea, these thoughts bringing a smile to my face. Everyone had retired for the day and the house was engulfed in darkness. I looked up as I saw the maid climbing down the stairs. Aariz had sent her. He was waiting for me in the room.

The room was a mess. Boxes of all sizes and knick-knacks were sprawled across the bed. One by one, he showed me what he had got from Chicago. I looked at him and nodded from time to time but my mind was somewhere else. I was thinking about the days Rehaan and I had spent together—the splash of water as we paddled across Regent's Canal; the gush of cold wind as we explored the streets of London on our bicycles; the pleasure of watching Rehaan swim in the pools of Hampstead Heath Park; and the calm silence that rested between us as we sat on the damp grass of the park. All of a sudden, I wanted to go back to these places and relive the moments we had created together.

'So did you like your gifts?' Aariz asked, bringing me back to the present.

'Um, yeah. I did. Thanks,' I said.

'I think this black lacy top will look really good on you. Why don't you put it on? I want to see if it fits,' he said, handing me the piece of clothing.

I looked at the top and then at him.

'You want me to wear it now?' I asked, raising a brow.

'Yes, now . . .' he said, leaning forward and caressing my cheeks. His touch did nothing for me. Gone were the days when my heartbeat accelerated by only looking at his face.

'Aariz,' I interrupted him. 'I . . . I'll wear this some other day. I am feeling really tired right now. In fact, you should also rest. It must have been a long day for you,' I told him, pushing his hand away.

'Are you sure?' he asked.

'Yes, let's call it a night.' I turned around and walked towards the bed.

∩

The next day, I waited impatiently for Aariz to leave for work. Rehaan had still not texted me the place and time and I looked at my phone every few minutes. *Would we continue to meet after today,* I wondered. Would Rehaan make a new itinerary or would I have to look for excuses to see him?

I had told Aariz about the plan and to remove any suspicion from his mind had also extended the invitation to him. But he had refused, giving work as the reason. His disinterest in my life did not affect me any more. Maybe things would have been different if we had a 'normal' relationship. Maybe he would have even objected to my meeting male friends.

Thankfully, my in-laws were also going out for a dinner party and wouldn't be back before midnight. I was beginning to enjoy this new-found freedom.

As evening approached, I decided to get ready. My phone beeped as I stepped out of the shower. I rushed to read the new message, thinking it might be from Rehaan. It wasn't. I dialled his number. There was no response. I tried again, but he didn't answer. Finally, after a few seconds, my phone screen flashed again. It was him.

Hey! I'm sorry but we have to cancel today's plan. I'm on a date with a very pretty girl. Tinder does work after all. I'll catch you tomorrow.

Blood rushed to my cheeks as I read his message. I felt jealous. He had chosen some random girl over me. How dare he? Was he trying to take revenge? I knew what the reason was. Aariz's sudden appearance and his display of affection had made Rehaan envious. A person like him could never mature or control his emotions. He was still the same. Feeling disappointed, I took the car keys and headed out to Soniya's place. I made a mental note to not meet him ever again. But the next day, when he called me, I couldn't say no. Though I was still quite angry, I did not express it. He asked me to meet him at the London Eye at 7 p.m.

🎧

I reached the London Eye right on time. When leaving home, I left my car and took the Tube. I knew if I did that, Rehaan would drop me back. On the way, I kept thinking of Rehaan and really looked forward to meeting him.

The London Eye stood magnificently against the sky filled with bright, blinking stars. I'd taken the ride of the giant Ferris wheel a lot of times but never with Rehaan.

I sent him a text as soon as I arrived and waited for his reply. It was a busy day, several tourists and locals had gathered for the beautiful experience. While I was watching the merry faces, a tap on my shoulder startled me. I turned around to see that it was Rehaan.

'Hey,' I said, my cheeks flushed with excitement. I couldn't deny the fact that I had missed him.

'Hey,' he said.

'You're late.'

'Yeah, I know. Was caught up with work.'

'So . . . err . . . how was your date last night?' I asked.

'Oh, yeah, it was good,' he said, nodding.

'How was the girl?' I asked nonchalantly.

'Pretty. In fact, very pretty!' he said dreamily.

'Really? Well, good for you,' I said, flashing a fake smile.

'Let's see how it goes.' He shrugged.

I felt a jab of envy.

'Okay, so you wait here. I'll go get our tickets for the ride.'

'Ride? Are we going up there?'

'Yeah, it'll be fun.' He patted my shoulder before walking towards the ticket counter.

The conversation had made me sulky. He should have invited that girl if he liked her so much. Why did he invite me?

'Let's go,' he announced, flashing the tickets.

I followed Rehaan to the queue which was filled with people of all kinds, all straining their necks to catch a view of the big wheel above them. Rehaan skirted the queue and we went through another entrance. He showed our tickets to the security personnel and after a short wait, we were ushered to a capsule in the wheel. To my amazement, we had the entire capsule to ourselves.

'Wow. That was quick,' I told him as the doors to our capsule shut. 'Did you get us a private capsule?'

He nodded as he looked at me, his hands resting on the railing.

'Nice.' I nodded, looking out of the glass windows. I had seen this view before but each time I marvelled at how breathtaking the city looked from the London Eye. John Legend sang 'All of Me' softly in the background.

'I know you must have been here a lot of times. I just wanted you to see the city at night. It looks so peaceful right now, so beautiful,' he said, standing close to me.

'Yes,' I whispered, as I glanced at him. 'It really does.'

'Zynah,' he said, his eyes boring into mine. 'Whenever I feel lonely, I come here.'

'You're not lonely,' I told him, giving him a sidelong glance.

'What makes you say that?' he asked in a low whisper, his breath caressing my skin. Till then, I had not realized how close we were standing.

'You have a girlfriend now,' I said.

He stared into my eyes for a few seconds and then burst out laughing.

'What happened? I wasn't joking.'

'She's not my girlfriend, Zynah. In fact, I don't have one.'

'But you just met someone yesterday and liked her.'

'I was lying. I didn't go out on any date.'

'What? Why did you lie and cancel our plan then?'

'Well, uh . . .' He thought for a few seconds. 'I don't know. It's really . . . really complicated.'

'Tell me, Rehaan! I want an answer. If you weren't busy yesterday, why did you cancel our plan?'

'Because I didn't want to face you!'

'What? Why?'

'I was jealous!'

'Of what?'

'Of your closeness with Aariz. I couldn't stand his arm around your waist and his lips on yours . . . I was pissed off.'

I pursed my lips as I took in his words. I didn't know what to say.

'But you know what, Zynah? You were right. I don't feel lonely any more because I have someone in my life. Someone who is always there for me. . .'

What was he implying?

'That someone is you.'

'Rehaan . . .' I blurted out.

'Aren't you with me?' he asked before I could finish.

'I am,' I said, reassuring him.

He chuckled.

'What?' I asked, amused at his reaction.

'Are you really with me, Zynah?' he asked, his expression becoming serious. There was no hint of amusement on his face.

'Yes,' I replied confidently.

'Sure?' He took another step towards me, shortening the distance between us. '

I nodded, looking into his eyes. Behind us, the Ferris wheel continued to rotate slowly, offering stunning views of the city. He slowly took my hand in his and leaned forward. My breath quickened.

'The truth is . . . you were never with me, Zynah. You never belonged to me. You weren't with me yesterday and you won't be with me tomorrow. The only thing we have is this moment right now,' he whispered slowly against my lips, caressing my cheek with the back of his hand. 'Only this moment.'

Oddly, his touch aroused me. For the first time I saw him in a new light. Not as a friend, but as someone who made my heartbeat quicken, who made me go weak in my knees, who sent a shiver down my spine. He held my hand, entwining our fingers together. I closed my eyes to feel the warmth of his touch.

I waited for him to embrace me in his arms or plant a kiss on my lips but none of that happened. In fact, he just stood there, looking at the view before us. I could hear his loud heartbeat and sense his uneven breathing. After he released my hands, I slowly opened my eyes to look at him. He continued looking outside the window, oblivious to what I was feeling. I heaved a sigh of relief; glad that he had not crossed his limits. However, I also felt a jab of disappointment. Did I want him to cross his limits? I felt ashamed at my thoughts. I was a married woman. I couldn't cheat on Aariz. I blinked back tears and looked away. It was me who had allowed this to happen. I shouldn't have come here in the first place. All of a sudden, I felt claustrophobic. I wanted to run away from this place, from this feeling, from these emotions that I had experienced just a few seconds ago. I did not want to get involved with Rehaan. He was my friend. My best friend. I had never been attracted to him. Then what had happened suddenly? Had I just developed these feelings or always had them deep down?

Rehaan

Throughout the remaining Ferris ride, a wall of silence fell between Zynah and me. I knew I'd done something I shouldn't have. I hadn't planned on expressing my feelings to her, even if indirectly. I had failed my resolve to never disclose my feelings to her or to let her see what she really meant to me. Perhaps I had offended her, but I knew I had not crossed my limits.

When the Ferris wheel came to a stop, Zynah exited the capsule in a hurry, leaving me behind. I hurried behind her, down the steps.

'Zynah, I'll drop you back!' I called out.

'It's okay, Rehaan,' she said, avoiding eye contact. 'I'll manage myself.'

I just stood there as she got into a taxi and left. I should have stopped her, held her hand and told her how much I loved her. But I didn't; I just let her walk away. I suddenly realized what I had done. Even without saying it, I had professed my love for her. I had to stop her before it was too late. It was a do or die situation.

I got into my car and drove straight to Mallord Street.
I took a shortcut and reached before her. After waiting
for around half an hour, I saw Zynah getting out of the
taxi and heading towards her house.

'Zynah!' I called out.

She slowed down when she heard me and turned to
look at me.

'What are you doing here?' she asked, a frown
appearing on her beautiful face.

'Look, I'm sorry, all right? I know I said something
I shouldn't have . . .' Honestly, I had no idea why I was
taking the entire blame on myself. This is not what I had
planned to say her.

'Rehaan,' Zynah said dismissively. 'I think you should
just go home. It's late. I don't want any trouble.' She turned
to walk away but I held her hand, stopping her.

'Please just listen to me once,' I pleaded, looking into
her eyes.

She looked at her hand for a few seconds and then
looked back into my eyes, her face softening. She sighed.

'Okay, hold on,' I said, taking a deep breath. 'Maybe
I shouldn't be apologizing for what I did. I think what I
said was right. I meant every word.'

'Rehaan?' she whispered.

'Zynah . . .' I held her hands firmly. 'Please leave him.
He doesn't deserve . . .'

'Wait,' she interrupted me. 'Don't say anything else.
Please.'

I sighed, my heart beating wildly.

'I don't think I can go through with this. I don't have
the courage to end my marriage. And I don't want to see
you ever again,' she said finally.

'What?' I whispered, shocked.

'Yes, Rehaan. Please do not contact me ever again.'

She freed her hand from my hold and walked towards her house. I stood glued to the spot as the reality dawned on me. She unlocked the door and stepped inside without even looking at me.

Had she broken my heart once again? My stomach churned in pain and bile rose at the back of my throat, burning it. I could not let her walk away. She didn't have the right to decide the course of my life. I had to stand up for myself and speak up. Without worrying about the consequences of my actions, I walked up to the main door. Thankfully, it was unlocked. I knew I was breaking in but I had no other option. I found Zynah in the living room, leaning against the fireplace with her hand on her forehead.

'Zynah?' I said, taking a few steps towards her.

'Rehaan?' She spun around, shocked to see me in the house. 'What the hell are you doing here? How dare you come inside without my permission?' she yelled.

'Listen to me, Zynah, I have to speak to you,' I said.

'Get out right now! Did you hear me? Get out!' she screamed but I didn't budge. Instead, I closed the distance between us and grabbed her arms.

Before I could say anything, a white man came out of one of the rooms—bare-chested, clad only in a pair of shorts.

'What's going on?' he asked.

Zynah froze and her eyes widened in shock. I didn't recognize him. Who was he? What was he doing here?

A few seconds later, a similar look dawned on his face as well. Shock or mortification, I couldn't comprehend.

'What happened?' Aariz asked, appearing in the doorway. He was as scantily clad as the other man. Now it was his turn to go white with shock.

'Zynah?' Aariz said in a low voice.

'You were . . . home?' she stammered, tears forming in her eyes.

It did not take me long to understand the situation. Both Aariz's parents and Zynah were out and expected back much later. So, he had called over his boyfriend for a dalliance at home. Zynah had caught him red-handed by returning early. I was horrified for Zynah and decided I would not leave her alone with him.

'Zynah,' I took her hand in mine. 'Let's go.'

'You go, Rehaan. I'll be there in a few minutes,' she said, her tear-filled eyes not moving from her husband and his boyfriend.

🎧

I did not like the idea of waiting outside for her. Why couldn't she just come with me? Was she still trying to reason with him? Even after what had happened? Had I been in her shoes, I would have walked away—from his house; from his life. Or smacked his face. The old Zynah would have definitely picked the latter option. But what was the new Zynah up to?

Twenty minutes passed but there was still no sign of her. I dialled her number but she did not answer. I wondered what was going on inside. Was she confronting him? Yelling at him? Or was he yelling at her for invading his privacy? But, how could he? He was the one who had purposely ruined her life. I was running out of patience. I could no longer stand out in the cold and wait for her as she fought her battle alone. Gathering my wits, I walked back to the house and reached for the door knob. But it was locked. Why? I pounded on the door but nobody came to open it. Suddenly, an irrational fear engulfed me.

Beads of sweat formed on my forehead as I contemplated the situation. I could not involve the police as that would only worsen things for Zynah. The only people I could think of calling were Zynah's parents. They had a right to know what was going on in their daughter's life. Without thinking about the consequences, I dialled her landline number.

'Hello?' Zynah's mother picked up.

'As-salaam-alaikum, Aunty, this is Rehaan, Zynah's friend,' I said.

'Wa-alaikum-salaam, beta. How are you? Is everything okay?'

'Aunty, I need to tell you something. It's about Zynah.'

'What about Zynah? Where is she?'

Without delving into the unnecessary details, I gave her a quick summary.

'Zynah and I were out for dinner. When we came back to her house, we found . . . she caught Aariz with someone else.'

'What do you mean with someone else, beta? Who was there?' She sounded worried.

'Aunty, I don't know if Zynah has told you about this or not but your son-in-law is gay . . . he is in a relationship with another man,' I said.

'What?' she whispered, shocked.

'Yes . . . and now she's inside the house with them and she's not answering my call or opening the . . .' Before I could complete the sentence, I heard a loud thud on the other end of the line and the call abruptly ended. I paused for a few moments to understand what went wrong. As I dialled the number again, the door opened and Zynah walked out—her face pale, pain-stricken and aghast.

'Zynah!' I called out. 'Are you okay?' I held her face in my hands and looked into her eyes.

'What did you say to my mother?' she asked, her voice breaking. 'What did you say to her on the phone just now?'

'Why, what happened?' I asked.

'Did you tell her about Aariz? Did you?' she screamed at me, pushing me back.

'Yes, I did! I had to! You were inside with him and you weren't answering my calls. I panicked and called your parents!' I shouted back at her.

'How dare you, Rehaan! How dare you call my parents and tell them everything? Who gave you this damn right?'

'But what happened?'

Right then, Aariz, now fully clothed, came out on to the porch, held Zynah by her shoulders and requested her to get inside the car.

'Let's go, Zynah. We should be there in no time.'

I switched my gaze from Zynah to Aariz and then back to Zynah, wondering what was going on.

'What happened?' I asked as Aariz escorted Zynah to the car.

'Thanks to you, my friend, Zynah's mother had a panic attack and she's been hospitalized,' Aariz snapped. 'Please excuse us now.'

Within seconds, they got into the car and drove off, leaving behind a cloud of dust.

Damn . . . what have I done? What have I done . . . Damn, damn, damn!

Zynah

I cried throughout the journey. I had never expected that Rehaan would disclose everything to my family, especially my mother. He knew that she had recurrent panic attacks. He had no right to tell her about Aariz. I swore on God I'd never forgive him if something happened to my mother. I looked at Aariz and felt a sharp pain in my chest. I had believed that he was changing for me, for himself, for our life but I was proved wrong. He was still in a relationship with the person he was in love with. What about those feelings that he said he'd developed for me? How could a person be in love with two people at the same time? I was a fool to have believed him. It was my mistake. I could not bring myself to accept his infidelity and while I was still grappling with these thoughts, I had found out about my mother's panic attack. This too had been my mistake—to believe that Rehaan could be a loyal friend. He was not. He could never be. Aariz had betrayed me. Rehaan had hurt me too. Neither of them deserved me.

I jumped out as soon as the car pulled into the hospital's driveway. Rushing towards the information desk, I asked for my mother.

'Zynah!' Daddy called out to me before the receptionist could fill me in with the details.

'Daddy?'

I turned to look at him and rushed into his arms.

'How's Mummy? What happened?'

'It was a panic attack . . . I was fortunate enough to bring her here on time,' he told me, gripping my hands tightly.

'Is she okay?' I asked, tears rushing down my face.

'Yes, she's absolutely fine now.'

'Thank God . . .' I whispered, closing my eyes.

'But Zynah . . . what Rehaan told us about Aariz . . .' he said, his voice trailing off.

I opened my eyes and looked at him, my body trembling.

'Is it true?' he continued.

'What are you saying?' I asked him in a whisper, shocked.

'Rehaan was here a few minutes ago and he told me everything about Aariz when I asked him.'

A flash of hurt appeared in his eyes when I did not defend Aariz. Rehaan had told my parents the truth, and I saw no point in denying it now. My silence had spoken for me.

'Zynah . . .' he gasped. 'Does this mean that it's true?'

I bit the inside of my cheek and nodded, fresh tears beginning to well up in my eyes. I turned away from my father's gaze.

'Zynah . . . why didn't you tell us . . . why?' he asked.

I looked back into his eyes. A lump formed in my throat as I forced myself not to break down.

'Do Kamran and Raima know about this . . . do they know?'

'Only Aunty knows,' I said slowly.

'Why did she keep this from us? Why?'

He frowned, anger filling his eyes.

I wiped away a tear that rolled down my cheek.

'And for how long were you going to keep this from us?' he asked.

A feeling of deep remorse made me turn away again.

'Oh God,' he said, shaking his head. 'I can't believe you have hidden this from us for so long. If it hadn't been for Rehaan, we would have never found out. I'm so grateful to that boy. Zynah . . . what were you thinking?' Disappointment flooded his face.

'Daddy, I'm sorry . . .' I whispered, choking.

'I swear I won't spare Kamran and his son,' he said, shaking his head.

'No! Daddy, no!'

I calmed him down by putting a hand on his shoulder.

'Please don't do anything. I promise we will sort it out. Please calm down for now.'

'Oh honey . . . how could we have been blind to what you were going through all this time . . .' he said, breaking down into tears.

'I'm sorry, Daddy . . . I'm so sorry,' was all I could whisper before I burst into tears. My father embraced me in his soothing arms and we both silently cried.

Uncle Kamran and Aunty Raima also came to the hospital to check on my mother. Aunty Raima sat beside me and comforted me. There was something different about her. She repeatedly apologized for allowing her son to marry me. She said it was a mistake to assume that Aariz would change after marriage. I looked at her in shock. What had brought this on? What had suddenly made her realize that she had been wrong about her son all along? She must have found out that my parents knew everything now. Aariz must have told her. I calmed her down and then walked up to Daddy and requested him to not get into an argument with my in-laws. He agreed and promised to hold his anger for the time being. Aariz walked out of the doctor's cabin and said that Mummy was fine now. We would be able to take her home within a few hours.

I took the doctor's permission and went to meet Mummy in the ward, where she was resting, and sat on the edge of the bed.

'Zynah . . .' she called out for me as soon as she realized I was sitting close to her.

'Mummy, I'm here,' I told her, smiling. 'Are you feeling any better now?'

'Are you feeling okay?' she asked, her voice sounding feeble.

I inhaled deeply before I replied, 'I'm fine. Don't worry about me. Everything is okay,' I reassured her, placing my hand on hers.

'But Rehaan told me something . . .' Her voice trailed off.

For a moment, I hesitated. I did not know what to say to her. Rehaan had told her the truth about Aariz but I did not know whether she had completely believed him. As I pondered on what to tell her, Daddy stepped into the room, closing the door behind him.

'Zee . . .' Mummy whispered. 'What have you gone through . . . why didn't . . . why didn't you tell us about Aariz?' A tear rolled down her eye.

'Mummy, everything is fine. Don't worry,' I said, wiping the tear off her cheek. 'I want you to rest.'

'My love, we won't let you suffer. You have to make the right decision . . . Do what's right for you . . .' she whispered.

'Yes, Zynah,' Daddy said. 'We won't let you compromise. It's never too late.'

Mummy locked her eyes with Daddy for a few seconds and then closed them. The effects of the sedative sent her into a deep slumber.

I held her hand firmly.

I will not compromise, Mummy. I'll do what's right for me. I'll make the right decision, I thought to myself.

🎧

A loaded silence hung in the air when I sat down next to Aariz on the bench, just outside Mummy's ward in the corridor. Neither did he speak to me nor did I initiate a conversation. I could feel his eyes on me. I knew he wanted to say something but he remained silent and so did I. Zayn called to check on Mummy while he was boarding a flight to London, and I reassured him that she was doing fine. A little while later, Daddy told me that we could take Mummy home. He had not said a word to either Aariz or his parents. He decided it would have to wait until Mummy fully recovered. I did not know how long he'd stay quiet though. I was afraid of his eventual reaction.

Daddy and I helped Mummy get into the car. Aariz trailed behind us.

'Zynah, come home with us. Right now,' Daddy ordered, shooting a dirty look at Aariz.

'Daddy, you take her home. I'll be there in a while,' I told him.

'But, Zee . . .'

'I'll be there, Daddy. Don't worry,' I said, reassuring him.

He nodded, still glaring at Aariz, and then got inside the car.

The car had just driven away when I saw Rehaan, who was standing across the parking lot.

Aariz tried to step in between us but I raised my hand and stopped him.

'Let me handle this,' I told him and walked over to Rehaan.

Rehaan

I was happy Zynah's mother had recovered from the panic attack. Otherwise, I'd have never forgiven myself. No matter what Zynah thought of me now, her father thanked me for telling them everything. I felt it was my duty to inform them. I did not care if Zynah hated me for this. I knew I had done the right thing. I stood outside the hospital and waited for her to come out. I had to talk to her. Suddenly, I saw Aariz, accompanied by two elderly people, making his way towards the main door. I recognized them as his parents. I did not want to miss this opportunity to speak to them, especially his mother, since she knew everything about her son. I walked resolutely in her direction and made my move.

'Ma'am, may I speak to you for a minute?'

'Yes?'

'I'm Zynah's friend, Rehaan. I don't know if she has ever mentioned my name . . .'

'Yes, of course, she has told me about you. How can I help you, son?'

'It's not me who needs help, Aunty. It's your son.'

'What?' A slight frown appeared on her face. 'What are you talking about?'

'You know very well what I'm talking about. Being a mother, you should accept your son for who he is and let him live his life. You thought marriage would change him but it hasn't. This has not only ruined Zynah's life but his as well.'

She opened her mouth to explain, but I interrupted her. 'I know it must be hard for you to accept that your son is gay. But think for a moment, apart from being your son, he is also a human being, a separate individual who has the right to choose his own life partner.'

'Look, son, I think this is . . .'

'Aunty, please, I request you to not make things difficult for Aariz and Zynah. Please accept him the way he is. Understand him. Respect his choices and let him be happy. Because of fear of rejection, because of you and Uncle, the societal pressure, Aariz and Zynah are not able to live the lives they want. They're compromising for a relationship which does not even exist. Please help them get out of this mess. Please.'

She considered my words for a moment. But then her husband called her, and she was forced to walk away. I sighed, wondering if my words had any effect on her.

I went back to my spot and continued to wait for Zynah. She, along with her parents, came out after an hour. I noticed that they were arguing—her father was asking her to come home with them but she wanted to go back with Aariz. This really annoyed me. Why did she still want to go back to him and his family? Now that her parents knew everything, she could easily end her relationship with Aariz and move on.

My heart skipped a beat when her eyes finally met mine. Slowly and tentatively, she made her way towards me. From the corner of my eye, I could sense that Aariz was looking at us.

'Zynah,' I whispered as she stood in front of me, looking into my eyes.

But she didn't say anything. When a few minutes passed and neither of us spoke, I decided to break the uncomfortable silence.

'I know what I did was not right but my intention was not to hurt you. What I did will hopefully set things right,' I said, my voice steady.

She bit her lower lip and looked away.

'You cannot live with that person any more, Zynah. He is not meant for you. You will just end up getting hurt.' I took a step forward, closing the distance between us. But she did not respond. I could see the hurt in her eyes, which were now filling up with tears.

'Forget about me, forget whatever happened between us, forget that we shared something special . . . but . . . but don't forget your self-respect, your life, your happiness,' I said. 'You deserve so much better.'

She choked back her tears.

'I know what I want and I know what I deserve,' she finally said. 'You don't have to tell me.'

I was reduced to silence.

'Zynah, we're getting late. We should leave now,' Aariz cut in.

I was dumbfounded.

'I'm coming,' Zynah said.

'Zynah?' I asked, looking at her.

'I have to go, Rehaan,' she said.

'With him?' I shot a quick glance at Aariz and then back at Zynah.

She nodded.

'After everything? You're still going with him? Why?' I asked, holding her shoulders.

'Because he's my husband!' She pushed me away and took a step back. I was shocked.

'Rehaan, look,' she said, sighing. 'I don't want to complicate the situation. I have made up my mind. I just . . . I just need to go right now. Please understand,' she told me.

I took a step back, my body feeling numb.

'You're my friend, right? My best friend? You are supposed to support me, strengthen my decision. Please do not weaken me, Rehaan, please don't!' She reached for my hand but I pushed her away. 'Rehaan?' she whispered, her pain-stricken eyes searching for mine.

I didn't look up to meet her gaze.

'Rehaan?' she said again.

'You've always walked out on me, Zynah,' but this time I won't let you do that,' I said, my voice low but determined.

'This time I'm walking out on you,' I declared. 'And I'm never coming back.'

'Rehaan? Please don't,' she said as tears streamed down her cheeks.

'All the best,' I said and walked away without looking back, and she didn't stop me.

PART FIVE

Rehaan

A Year Later
London, UK

When I was a kid I always used to wonder if I'd ever get a chance to showcase my work, my photographs, to the rest of the world. Shifting to London for my higher education had changed my life in many ways. After years of struggle, I finally had my own photography studio in London and was among the most popular contemporary artistes of the metropolis. And now I was finally having my own photography exhibition at The Photographers' Gallery. I had done exceptionally well as far as my professional life was concerned. My family was also happy with my progress. Azaan had shifted to London to complete his bachelor's programme and was staying with me.

Last month, I had surprised my parents with flight tickets to the UK. It was a family reunion and I was happy to see everyone I loved in the same room. Everything was going fine until Amma brought up the topic of my marriage. I bought time by telling her that I wasn't ready for a long-term commitment. She was not convinced but did not pursue the matter as she knew it would just lead to an argument.

It was the day of the exhibition. Some of my best works till date were on display. Except for one—a candid shot of Zynah riding a bicycle. The picture was quite close to my heart, and I did not want anyone to own it, except for me. She might have chosen someone else over me, but the truth was, I was still not able to forget her. At first she had lived in my memories, but now she dominated my thoughts, overpowering every aspect of my life.

'Rehaan, do you have a minute?' Hassan, my co-worker, asked, bringing me back to the present.

'Yeah, sure, what is it?' I asked.

'I think we have a problem. There's a customer who is insisting on buying the picture which is not for sale.'

'What?' I asked, frowning.

'Yes, I did explain that it wasn't for sale but he's not listening. He said he's willing to pay double the price.'

'Double or triple, who cares? Just tell him it's not for sale,' I said with a wave of my hand.

'I did but he's still insisting. Why not consider it? He's paying double,' Hassan said.

'Who is he? Send him in. I'll deal with him,' I told him.

'Sure.' Hassan walked out to get the guy.

∩

I was curious to see who this person was. Why would anybody want to purchase Zynah's picture at double the cost unless they knew her? I gulped down my coffee and prepared myself to meet this person.

'Rehaan?' someone called out.

I was taken aback to find Aariz standing in front of me, looking as handsome as ever in a light grey dress suit.

'Aariz?' I asked, furrowing my brows.

'I'm glad you recognized me,' he said, smiling.

'How could I ever forget you?' I mumbled.

'Your work is amazing. I was actually quite impressed. You have an eye for detail.'

His presence reminded me of Zynah. Had she also come along? Where was she? Was she outside, looking at the pictures? Did she and Aariz insist on buying her portrait together?

'Is that why you came here? To praise my photography skills?' I raised a brow.

'Actually, I have been meaning to meet you. I didn't know how to contact you but then I read about your upcoming exhibition in the newspaper.'

'Why were you so keen on meeting me?' I asked, folding my arms. 'Why are you here?'

He looked at me for a split second and then turned his gaze. I noticed a twinge of uneasiness on his face.

'I want to buy her portrait,' he finally said.

'It's not for sale. I believe you already know that.'

'But I really want it.'

'Has Zynah come with you?' I asked, changing the subject.

He became silent for a while, looking at his hands.

'Where's Zynah?' I asked him again.

'Don't you know?' he asked, looking at me.

'Why should I bother?' I shrugged. 'She never cared for me, so why should I?'

'You were her best friend, Rehaan. You should be by her side. You should support her more than anyone else,' he said.

'What?' I stifled a laugh. 'Support her more than her husband?'

'I'm not her husband any more, Rehaan. She left me,' he declared, sighing.

The words gave me a jolt of shock.

'What?' I asked. 'What do you mean she left you?'

'It was a mutual decision. We got divorced a couple of months ago.'

🎧

As my brain processed the sudden revelation, Aariz asked me to sit with him so he could fill me in on the details. He ordered himself a cup of coffee but I was too dazed, confused and furious to drink or eat anything.

'I can't believe this,' I said, continuing the conversation. 'How did this happen?'

'It was I who had forced her to continue in that meaningless relationship. I took advantage of her feelings and pleaded with her to stay. But the truth was she did not deserve a person like me who could not reciprocate her feelings. Yes, I did love her but not enough for a marriage. I had those feelings for someone else,' he explained.

'But how did things change?' I asked.

'In the beginning I was afraid to tell my family the truth. I didn't know how they'd react. I thought they'd not understand me and hate me forever. The night you and Zynah came home and found me with my boyfriend,' he paused, 'that's when Zynah decided to leave me.'

This was news to me.

'Zynah had made up her mind to leave me even before you called her mother. She told me she was going to file for a divorce.'

I looked down, recalling that night.

'I did not defend myself and agreed. I knew I had been lying to her all these months. I could never change myself. I could never give her what she deserved. It was better if we called it quits.'

'Does . . . does your father know about you?' I managed to speak.

'Yes. After Zynah's mother recovered, she came to our place with her parents. She asked me to tell my parents everything, especially my father. I hesitated at first, but she encouraged me. She said she would support me no matter what. I went up to my parents and told them the truth. I told them I was gay; that I was involved with someone else; that I had agreed to marry Zynah because of societal pressures. My mother was not convinced and said I should give my marriage another shot. But I stood my ground and told her that I couldn't be with any woman, let alone Zynah. I apologized to them and her family for lying, but I did not apologize for being homosexual. Because that's who I am. And I am not ashamed of it.'

'What happened next?' I asked, curious.

'My parents didn't know how to respond. So, they put the matter in Zynah's hands. She took the right decision and said we should get a divorce. Thanks to her, my parents are not angry with me any more. They eventually accepted me for who I am.'

'Where is she?' I asked.

'She has moved to Manchester. She got a job with a leading design firm and they wanted her to join as soon as possible.'

'Manchester? But what about her family?' I asked.

'They're still here, in London.'

I bit my lip, wondering how she did it all alone.

'You should have been there for her, Rehaan. You should not have abandoned her. You weren't there when she needed you the most.'

'Yeah, right,' I snorted. 'I've always been there for her, but she never wanted me. She always pushed me away.'

'Because she was in a relationship with me. She had her limitations.'

'I asked her . . . when I saw her outside the hospital . . . I asked her what she wanted but again she chose you . . . She wanted to be with you. I told her I would never come back . . . but that didn't change her decision,' I said, my voice trailing off.

'She had to settle things with me first, that's why she stayed back. You should have understood her,' Aariz said.

With my elbows resting on the coffee table, I covered my face with my hands to hide the tears streaming down my cheeks.

'She was a totally different person around you, Rehaan. You made her so happy.'

I wiped my cheeks with the back of my hand and looked away.

'I'm glad she has someone like you in her life. You're her anchor, her support, her best friend. What you share with her is immeasurable.'

'I cannot be there for someone who doesn't want me. I cannot,' I snapped, and stood up.

'She needs you, Rehaan. Perhaps, you won't realize this now but one day you will. And I hope it's not too late when you do.'

I folded my arms across my chest as I considered what he had said, my eyes still moist.

'Anyway, thanks for your time. I wish you all the luck. I should take your leave now.'

'No, wait!' I said, turning around.

'Yes?' he asked, looking at me.

'Can I . . . can I have her address?' I asked, my voice low.

His face lit up with a grin.

'Only on one condition,' he said.

'What?'

'I want you to sell me her portrait.'

'I've already told you it's not for sale,' I said.

'Fine, then I'm not giving you her address.' He turned his back on me.

'But why are you so keen on buying her picture? Why now?' I asked, irritated by his behaviour.

'Well.' He looked at me again, folding his arms. 'I want to buy this portrait on your behalf and send it to her so she knows it's taken by the person who deserves her the most.' He smiled.

I took in his words and then heaved a sigh. As I smiled back at him weakly, a tear of relief escaped my eye.

Zynah

Aariz and I parted ways a couple of months back. I was happy it all ended on a good note. I wouldn't say the conversation with his parents was easy. They felt ashamed, embarrassed, but I told them to stay strong. Aunty Raima apologized for rebuffing our earlier attempts to tell her the truth. I asked his parents for only one thing—to accept Aariz for who he was. He was still their son who had made them proud by securing a gold medal at his university; he was still the son who gave up his promising career in Canada to look after his family business in London; he was still the same son who gave up the person he loved to marry the girl of his parents' choice because he couldn't make them unhappy. I told them that I could not spend my life with someone whose feelings were divided. I gave our relationship another chance after I found out about him, but later realized we were just fooling each other.

Uncle Kamran, Aunty Raima, and even Aariz wanted me to resume working in their company but I politely refused. I wanted to get away from all this to explore my options and contemplate my life. So when an opportunity to work in a leading design firm in Manchester presented itself, I could not say no. I moved to Manchester as soon as the divorce was settled. Leaving my past behind paved way for a better future, for better days, where there was no darkness. I could breathe freely I was only responsible for myself and that feeling was liberating. I was happy that I had stood up for myself, that I had mustered up the courage to start afresh and become self-reliant. I felt like my old self again—light-hearted and happy-go-lucky. The episode with Aariz had brought a great deal of pain, but I had bounced back. I didn't know I had it in me to live independently. There was a time when Aariz meant the world to me; when I couldn't even think about a life without him. But that had changed. I still loved him but I was no longer *in love* with him. Perhaps, I never was. Rehaan was right about one thing. I did not love him. I only loved the idea of him.

As far as Rehaan was concerned, I was not in touch with him. He had blocked my number on his cell phone as well as on WhatsApp. Later I realized that I had not even added him on Facebook. I did try to get in touch with him but in vain. I tried to look up his studio on Google to get an address or a landline number but then I realized I'd never asked him the name. I missed him terribly. He'd always been there for me but I had always pushed him away. After this episode, I realized he was more than just a friend. I realized I had feelings for him. But I was glad he had decided to break all contact and stay away. A selfish, self-centred person like me could only bring unhappiness. I'd always broken his heart, belittled his emotions. I didn't deserve his friendship, let alone his love. I knew he had made no attempt to look for me in all these months. This pained me but I didn't blame him for it. I respected his decision.

I had finally moved on and settled in my new life. I shared an apartment with a girl named Julia who worked in a bank. She was sweet and usually kept to herself. This gave me plenty of time and space for self-reflection.

🎧

After a busy week, I finally found some time to unwind. It was a Saturday but Julia had to work overtime, so I had the apartment to myself. I'd already decided how to spend my weekend—wear pyjamas, make myself fettuccine Alfredo and then binge-watch all the episodes of *Game of Thrones*. That's what my ideal weekend usually looked like. As I was preparing the white sauce for the pasta in the kitchen, the doorbell rang. I rinsed my hands and walked up to the door to unlock it. There was no one outside. I was about to close the door when my eyes fell on a large package kept against the wall. I craned my neck to see who had left it and caught a fleeting glimpse of someone rushing down the stairs. *Might have been the delivery guy*, I thought.

There was no name on the small note pasted neatly on the box, except my name and address.

'Who sent me this?' I whispered to myself.

I somehow managed to drag it into my living room. After struggling with the brown wrapping paper for ten minutes, I pulled out a black-and-white portrait of myself. I took a few steps back to look at the gigantic picture. Memories from that time came flooding back and I was transported to another time—Rehaan and I cycling through the streets of London, giggling, soaking up the sun. I remembered that day vividly. I also remembered

that the photographer had caught me unawares. I knew
who he was. I knew *him*.

As the realization dawned on me, I dropped everything
and ran as fast as my legs could carry me out of the door
and down the stairs. I looked around, my frantic eyes
searching for him. But he was nowhere to be seen.

'Damn. . . . ' I hissed, letting out an exhausted gasp.

'Looking for a ride?' I heard someone say from
behind.

My face broke into an involuntary smile and I quickly
turned around.

Rehaan stood a few feet away from me, grinning.

Rehaan

'Ride?' she asked, hiding her smile. 'Why, Captain? Have you started driving Uber in Manchester as well?' Clad in pyjamas and a loose T-shirt, her hair tied up in a bun, she looked at me incredulously.

'Yeah, you can say that,' I said, shrugging.

She stifled a giggle, covering her mouth with her hand.

'Did you like the portrait?' I asked.

'Yes, but I like the photographer more,' she said with a coy smile.

Her confession made me smile. By the time I took a few steps in her direction, her eyes had turned moist. Her presence soothed my senses. I was a fool to leave her in the first place.

'I thought you were not going to come back,' she said, trying to hold back her tears.

'But I always do, right?' I said, sighing. 'I always come back for you, Zynah.'

'Why?' she asked. 'I don't deserve you. I've always caused you pain, made you suffer. I have hurt you, Rehaan. I'm not a good person.'

'I'm not a good person either. I left you when you needed me the most. I should have waited till you had made a decision.'

'Do you know, about the . . . divorce?' she asked, her brows creasing.

'Yes,' I nodded, adding, 'Aariz met me and told me everything. I'm proud of you, Zynah. I'm proud that you made the right decision and stood up for yourself. Aariz seems to be in a happy space now. You have changed his life.'

Hearing me say this, she smiled.

'I didn't change his life; he changed mine,' she said. 'I would have never realized what I was really missing out on if he hadn't come into my life. He made me realize who I really was. Most importantly, who I should be with.'

I smiled and held her hand. She looked at our hands and smiled back at me.

'You know what I feared the most? Living without him and getting a divorce. But the day I realized these were mere fears, I set him free and, in the process, liberated myself.'

I continued to look into her eyes, her hand firmly held in mine.

'So thank you for coming back and making me realize that I could stand up for myself and live my dreams.'

'Don't thank me. Thank yourself. You're the one who fought for yourself. Only you,' I said.

She nodded with a smile.

'Should we go inside? I'm sorry I didn't offer . . .'

'Wait,' I said, interrupting her. She looked at me, surprised.

'Can I say something first?' I asked, raising a brow, a playful smile on my lips.

She nodded, her eyes twinkling with happiness.

'I did say it a long time ago but perhaps you did not listen,' I added.

'I'm sorry for not listening. Please say it now.'

'I love you, Zynah Malik. I love you very much. I have loved you since the moment I laid eyes on you back in school. You're my inspiration. You're my world. You're . . . you're everything I have ever dreamed of,' I told her.

'That's it?' she asked, a tear escaping her eye.

'Um, I guess. Why, what happened?' I asked. 'Did I say something wrong?'

'No! This is the first time you've said it right!' She quickly drew closer to me, wrapped her arms around my neck and locked her lips with mine.

I took a step back and held her firmly by her waist. The kiss deepened, sending an electric jolt across my body. I didn't know kissing Zynah would be such an experience. We broke the kiss when we realized a small crowd had gathered around us. Before I could process what had happened, Zynah burst out laughing. Seeing her reaction, I couldn't hold myself back and started laughing too. I leaned closer to her and held her face in my hands. She looked at me longingly as I kissed her forehead. With her eyes closed, she leaned towards me for an embrace. I hugged her back, my lips grazing her hair. There couldn't be a happier moment in my life. I had Zynah in my arms. What else could I have asked for? I might have just got her in my life but she always had all of my heart.

Acknowledgements

Whenever I have to write the acknowledgements section of a book, I'm consumed with an overwhelming feeling because I have so many people to thank. I would not be here if it were not for these people—my parents and my siblings, especially my younger sister, Ayesha. She has been a constant support and will always remain my first reader and critic.

I am blessed to have worked with some incredibly talented people at Penguin Random House India: Tarini, my editor, who has been supportive, accommodating and appreciative since the beginning of my career; Peter Modoli, my publicist, who is always there when I need him; Meena Rajasekaran, who has, once again, designed a beautiful cover for this book; and Saloni Mital, who has been the best copy editor I could have asked for.

I would also like to express my gratitude to all those people who have been a part of my journey: my friends, colleagues, authors, readers, fans and well-wishers.

I want to thank everyone who ever said anything positive to me or taught me something. I heard it all, and it meant something. Trust me.

Finally, I want to thank Allah—without Him I wouldn't have been able to do any of this.